The characters and events in this book are fictiti
living or dead, is coincidental and not intended

Copyright © 2024 by Mike Salt
Cover Art © 2024 by BRAIN DEAD THREAD CO.
Edited by Meriah Gutterson at Marked Up Editing

Abomination Media supports the right to free expression and the value of copyright. The purpose of copyright is to encourage writers and artists to produce creative works that enrich our culture. We thank you for purchasing an authorized copy of this book. We appreciate your support of the author's rights.

No part of this book may be reproduced, redistributed, or resold without the author's permission.

The Publisher is not responsible for websites (or their content) that is not owned by the publisher.

ISBN: (Paperback) 9798324765057

All rights reserved.

PRAISE FOR
THIS ALL ENDS HORRIBLY

"A Splatterpunk lover's dream, Salts newest rips along at a million miles an hour, bludgeoning the characters – and readers – relentlessly, until we reach the horribly perfect ending."

-Steve Stred, 2X Splatterpunk nominated author of *Mastodon* and *Churn the Soil*

"A high speed house of horrors with all the blood and guts you expect from splatter horror with a healthy dose of heart-wrenching emotion. In THIS ALL ENDS HORRIBLY the story lives up to its name and Mike pours plenty of salt into your emotional wounds."

-Wendy Dalrymple, author of *White Ibis* and *Girls Night Out*

"Salt unleashes the sinister musings of his mind as he drops you into the hellscape of haunted suburbia. This All Ends Horribly is a visceral nightmare right up to the last page."

-Jennifer Osborn, author of *Intrusive Thoughts and Other Dark & Unusual Tales*

"As gruesome as it is fast-paced, THIS ALL ENDS HORRIBLY shows the strength of Mike Salt's writing. He doesn't hold back, and neither should you from picking this one up."

-Michael R. Goodwin, author of *Smolder*

"This All Ends Horribly blows into action like a literary hand grenade and never lets up the feverish fast pace. The whole book is like the explosive final scene of a movie, and like asphyxiation will take your breath away with satisfaction!"

-Jim Ody, author of *Little Miss Evil*

"The most impressive thing about the book is that it is relentlessly gruesome without it dampening the effect in any way. If you're expecting to stop for a breather, it isn't going to happen. There's no need to build suspense where we're going - this is a brutal, frantic, gruelling read, and Salt is the captain of a ship that's taking a nosedive straight to hell."

-MJ Mars, author of *The Suffering*

"What Mike Salt delivers isn't a gut punch, it's an axe straight to the head as you discover a true gruesome nightmare come to life."

-Chaz Williams, author of *Family Til' It can't Be, Gang Til' It Ain't*

"What do you get when Cabin in the Woods meets middle-class suburbia? You get 'This All Ends Horribly'. Mike Salt has written a haunted house book unlike any I've ever known. It is fast paced from the the very first page to the last. It absolutely terrified (and entertained) me from beginning to end."

-Asia Brito Guerrero, author of *Butterscotch*

"This book chains you down and won't let you go until you bite off your own arms. What a show-stopping, can't-sleep-at-night-inducing, WTF kind of contribution by Mike Salt. It'll scare your pants off."

-Cassandra Celia, author of *Sugarcane*

"This story is action-packed, grabbing you by the throat and not letting go until the last chapter. Mike was able to accomplish a lot in just over one hundred pages, causing me to feel anger, grief, and even some humor."

-Timothy King, author of *Seven Rabbits*

"Mike Salt's new book will get under your skin and send pins and needles all the way down to your toes... read at your own risk."

-Danielle DeVor, author of *The Marker Chronicles*

"This All Ends Horribly is more extreme than his other works, the random (very random) Mike Salt humor is peppered throughout, even when things are going... well... horribly."
        -Matt Micheli, author of *Pornageddon* and *Two Minutes with the Devil*

"Salt weaves a tapestry that is a brutal, bloody, splatterfest of pain and gore, then hangs it on a wall of dread and loss."
        -Kalvin Ellis, author of *In The Hills Above The Gristmill*

"I may be scarred for life but it was worth it. Utterly amazing."
        -J.L.E, author of *What Happens In The Woods*

"Mike delivers a fresh take on the horrors a haunted house can bring."
        -Z. Martin, author of *The Price of Insanity*

"This book goes from 0-100 in just a few blood soaked pages. A gore soaked rollercoaster ride from start to finish."
        -Richard Beauchamp, author of *Triptych: Three Tales of Frontier Horror*

"Each step of the way, you find yourself wondering what comes next... and how much worse it can get. I assure you, it does get worse."
        -Nikolas P. Robinson, Splatterpunk nominated author of *Beneath The Unspoiled Wilderness*

"Absolutely no one is safe for even one second, it's like one big elongated scream and I loved it."
        -Ben Young, author of *Stuck*

"From the opening page, Salt drops the reader right into the belly of the beast and never lifts his boot from the pedal... this is the next chapter in true horror."
        -J.B. Arnold, author of *Exit 202*

BOOKS BY MIKE SALT

A LINKVILLE HORROR SERIES

Damned to Hell – Darklit Press

The Valley – Darklit Press

The House on Harlan – Darklit Press

Hollow – Darklit Press

STANDALONE NOVELS

Price Manor: The House that Burns

THIS ALL ENDS HORRIBLY

AUTHOR OF THE LINKVILLE HORROR SERIES

MIKE SALT

THIS ALL ENDS HORRIBLY

MIKE SALT

ABOMINATION MEDIA

This story has elements that may be considered triggers for some individuals... If you think you might be one of these people, go to the back of the book and understand what you are in for.

Beware of spoilers.

CHAPTERS

Prologue	1
One.	6
Two.	12
Three.	20
Four.	28
Five.	36
Six.	46
Seven.	56
Eight.	64
Nine.	72
Ten.	76
Eleven.	84
Twelve.	92
Thirteen.	102
Fourteen.	106
Fifteen.	116

Dedicated to a certain group of friends that have done Monday dinners at my hizzy for the last 6 years.

Final bets on who dies first?

PROLOGUE

"I can't do it," Diana said, her fingers trembling as she tried to pull a cigarette out of the pack and move it to her mouth. "It doesn't feel right."

Cameron turned to her, looked her up and down, then faced the road again as his hands tightened around the steering wheel. "We don't have a fucking choice, unless you want Adam to die."

Together they drove through the night, trying to make up as much distance as possible. The majority of the car ride was spent watching his rearview mirror and listening to Diana itch from the seat beside him. He could smell the car fill with the sweat and body odor from the last few days. The white tank-top that Cameron was wearing was the same one he slipped on three mornings ago. However, the stark white was replaced with a dull gray and brown, with splashes of red that no one would confuse with anything besides blood. The last three days had been unexplainable. Even if they managed to pull this task off, there was no guarantee that life would be better. How would they explain the dead bodies? How would they explain their house being splattered with blood and ancient torture weapons? Would they all disappear when they were done? Could everything go back to normal?

Cameron rubbed his eyes as the exhaustion started to catch up to him.

"I need to pee," Diana said as she continued to itch at an already open wound that had only grown further down her leg as the days passed.

Usually, Diana and Cameron didn't spend as much time together, so he didn't really know how horrible it was to hang out with her. Hell, if it wasn't for Stan bringing this whole thing down upon them, she wouldn't have been with Cameron anyway. There was no way around it, all of this fell on Stan's shoulders. None of this would have happened if Stan didn't bring the same box that now sat in the backseat of Cameron's '84 Plymouth over. Cameron shook his head as the idea of Stan not coming over that night flooded his mind. How different things would have been. Stan would still be alive instead of splattered against the wall of Cameron's home in the trailer park. So would Nico. Gem too.

"I need to piss," Diana said again, the irritation in her voice making Cameron grit his teeth.

Cameron continued down the highway, with no idea how far they had driven; but he was sure that time was running out. "How much longer do we have?" He asked as he flipped the blinker and slowed the vehicle to turn off the highway.

"I. Need. To. Piss."

As Cameron turned to Diana and raised a hand, he felt the rage inside his blood boil as his instinct to swipe the back of his hand down on her tried to take over. Cameron wasn't proud of it, but it wouldn't have been the first time he put his hands on a woman... probably wouldn't be the last time either. Instead, Cameron tried to calm himself, and brought his hand back down. He ran his fingers through his thinning, dirty hair. He could feel the grime and sweat stick to his fingers. The clots of blood that had dried on top of sweat over his blonde curls. "Diana," he said calmly, "how long have we been driving?"

Diana looked through glaring eyes as she fumbled around her legs blindly, searching for her phone. This wasn't the first time that a man had raised a hand to her, Cameron was positive of that. Hell, he had seen it first hand last month. Stan had smacked her a *good one* as they hung out, drank beers, and smoked. Cameron couldn't remember what it was about, but he remembered chuckling as Diana spit blood in Stan's dumb face.

"It's been two hours and fifty-three minutes," Diana said with a soft voice.

"Okay, okay, okay," Cameron repeated to himself. "Let's just find some place to do it. We don't have much time."

Diana lowered her head and Cameron could hear her softly begin to cry.

"It's not murder, Diana. They will have a fair chance, just like we did. We won't be killing them."

"It is killing them if they *die*!" Diana screamed.

"They will have plenty of time! We didn't have the same amount of time!"

"Yes, we did!" Diana continued to yell.

"No, we didn't," Cameron tried to keep his tone low and soft. Last thing they needed with only a couple minutes left was for him to lose his temper. "We were all too *fucked* up the first night. We didn't hear the rules. When things started happening we just thought 'wow, we are all really fucking high right now'. So no, we didn't have a fair shake of things."

Diana looked out the window as Cameron pulled into a stereotypical suburban neighborhood. Two story houses, painted boring colors. Nice fences that kept dogs or strangers off their immaculate flowerbeds. Even in the darkness of night, with only a cloud covering the moonlit night, Cameron could see the brightly colored flowers in front of neatly manicured houses.

Cameron could feel something deep inside him rise. It wasn't hate, but it also *kinda* was. Had he grown up in a house like this, could he have had a better life? Instead of a single-wide full of empty beer cans and vodka bottles, could a house with two parents and a healthy relationship have changed everything for him? Maybe he would be in a loving relationship with a gorgeous woman instead of constantly alone. Maybe he would play golf on the weekends and share a beer at the clubhouse instead of sharing a spoon and a lighter on a disgusting couch in his trailer.

"How do we choose?" Diana asked as they drove down the block. She looked down to the timer on her phone. "Five minutes."

"Look for a house that has at least two cars in their driveway," Cameron said. "If a light is on, that would be better. We need someone, anyone, to be home."

A couple seconds passed by before Diana pointed a finger out her window, "There."

Cameron turned and looked over at the greenish-blue house. A white sedan and red mustang were out front. The window facing the street cast a blue light that moved; someone was watching TV. "Perfect," Cameron said. He turned around and grabbed the cardboard box from the back seat. His fingers tingled as they touched the surface. Something inside his brain screamed for him to *drop it*. He knew what was inside… and what it was capable of. He pulled it back to himeslf and handed it towards Diana.

"Fuck you," she said. "No, I'm not killing this family." She crossed her arms.

"Do it," Cameron insisted as he pushed the box against her arms.

"No," she said. "I won't." She looked down to her phone. "Two minutes."

Cameron opened his mouth to say something. The rage building up in his veins started to climb again, until the reality of the situation set in. It didn't matter who did it, just as long as *someone* did. "Fucking pussy." Cameron said as he climbed from the car.

He walked down the driveway of the house, cautious as to any movement inside the windows. Cameron took a step forward, holding his breath as he moved.

A bright light illuminated the area; a motion activated spotlight.

Cameron froze.

He looked back to the vehicle, seeing Diana shoo him towards the house, her mouth clearly saying: *go*.

Cameron walked over to the front door, placing the small cardboard box in the center of a welcome mat that read: This house is full of kids and dogs. Love. Hugs. Nachos.

Cameron smirked at the mat, reading the words over and over.

They were a family. With a couple of kids, at least. Maybe an animal or two. They had, at the very least, a welcome mat's degree of humor. They were real.

He felt guilty.

Cameron reached back down to retrieve the package that was no bigger than a shoebox. His fingers hovered over it for a moment before he pulled them back. He couldn't. It was already done. Even if he had enough time to get it away, he wouldn't have enough time to take it across the street or next door.

"I'm sorry," Cameron said as he walked backward, away from the door. The motion activated light exploded once again, casting a long shadow over Cameron as he covered his face with his right hand. He looked up to the window with the TV glowing, "I'm fucking sorry."

Cameron felt a tear slip down his face as he approached his car, using the backside of his hand to wipe it away. He pulled the door handle to the car up and stepped into the vehicle.

Diana didn't turn towards him.

She sat and looked out the window towards the house. "Did we do the right thing?" She asked. "What did we do?"

"We didn't have a choice," Cameron said. "As long as they open the box and listen to the instructions within the first day, they'll be fine. We didn't know the rules until the third day."

"And look how that turned out," Diana said as she placed a cigarette in her mouth. She brought a white lighter to the tip of the cigarette and flicked it to life. In the light of the flame Cameron could see the blood soaked bandage wrapped around her hand, covering the stubs that used to be her pinky and ring finger.

"They'll be fine," Cameron asserted. "They just have to fucking pay attention. It starts slow the first couple days. They just need to notice it before it gets out of control."

Diana chuckled as she sucked in a long breath through the cigarette.

"They just can't wait. They need to open it by tomorrow, at the latest. They'll be fine," Cameron said. "They just can't wait. They'll be fine, as long as they Just. Don't. Wait."

He pulled the gear into Drive and pulled the car around, back in the direction they came from. "Everything will be fine. They just have to open it right away."

CHAPTER ONE

THIS ALL ENDS HORRIBLY | 6

THREE DAYS LATER

The black minivan cruised down the highway. The atmosphere inside the van was thick with exhaustion, and everyone was just anxious to get out of the van.

Derek had taken the last stretch of the drive, letting the rest of the group sleep off their various stages of hangovers. The melody of The Beach Boys quietly singing "Help Me Rhonda" lingered from the front speakers. He pressed his finger down on a button on the door, the glass slowly inching down. The cold, fresh air in his face would help keep him awake on this final stretch home.

In the corner of his vision, he saw Carissa readjust in her seat. She grabbed the seat belt and pulled it away from her as she rolled her body to get comfortable. He smiled and looked back to the road. It had been a long trip, it would be a shame if something were to happen when they were almost home.

"Where we at?" A groggy voice said from behind him.

Derek adjusted the mirror and found Tyler stretching in the middle row, "Just outside of town. Shouldn't be that much longer."

"Fucking finally," Tyler said as he leaned his head back against the window and closed his eyes.

The idea of a trip to Disneyland seemed like a good idea on paper. That was until they were standing in the blistering heat all day, after staying out all night; filling their bellies full of vodka and whiskey. It was the girls' idea to go on the trip. The group of seven made it a mission to go on two vacations together every year. One with all of their children (Derek and Carrissa having two, just like Tyler and Flea. However, Thomas and Shawna packed a large herd of four all by themselves. Loki was the odd man out, with no significant other, and having no children to bring on these trips.) Then, a second trip that would be just for the adults. A chance to drink heavily, laugh, and do it again the next couple of days. In the past they had found themselves renting beach houses or traveling to a bigger city and drinking at breweries. However this time, the girls wanted to go "all out". They had done a Disneyland trip the year prior with the kids, and thought it would be incredible to have the same experience without a gaggle of children to look after. They weren't wrong, it was fun, but it was also a lot more exhausting than any of them had thought it would be. At the end of the trip, the five days spent together were going to be etched into their memories for a long time and the twelve hour drive home would be miserable. The trip was filled with inside jokes and ammunition to haunt one another for years. Stories about who was *so drunk* that they fell down a flight of stairs or who tried to climb a tree and acted like a squirrel. Bonding moments that weren't manufactured or put in a box. At one point one of the girls even talked to the group about a traumatic experience. Something she hadn't told anyone about. A time where she found herself alone in a bar, before she was even old enough to be in one, and the bartender had made her a "special drink." However, at the end of the night she was barely walking and woke up the next day confused and naked. She never talked about it, but was adamant that no one should ever enter the stupid dive bar simply called Yee-haw Beer Barn. The group grew closer that night when she was vulnerable enough to share such a traumatic experience with them. They didn't need to talk about it, the fact that she finally opened up was enough.

"Babe, wake up," Thomas said from the back row.

Derek heard small moans of disapproval as the rest of the van began to wake up. Soon the van was filled with people stretching and yawning, making noises that sounded pathetic and overly exaggerated.

"We there yet?" Carissa asked through her own yawn beside him.

Derek reached out and grabbed her hand, lifting it to his face and kissing it. "Almost. Was gonna let you sleep the rest of the way, but someone decided to wake the entire group." Derek shot a look into the mirror.

Thomas shrugged, "What?"

"Dude, I was having the best dream. I was–or we were– fuck, I forgot what was happening now," Loki said. "Something to do with Disneyland and a pirate. I can't recall."

"There were pirates at Disneyland," Carissa said.

The entire van fell quiet for a moment before bursting out in laughter.

"No, shit," Tyler said between laughs. "I think we all know that. It is literally one of the most famous rides of all theme parks."

Carissa sank down into her seat, crossing her arms and scrunching her face, "I was just saying."

"Oh honey," Derek patted her on the head. "They are just fucking with you."

"Whatever," Carissa said, "I just want to get home and see the babies."

"Well, we can pick them up in the morning," Derek said. "No use waking them up and pulling them out of bed this late."

"That's our plan too," Shawna said. "I just want to get home so I can crash. Picking the babies up is *tomorrow-me's* problem."

Derek looked into the mirror at Tyler, "What about you guys?"

Flea pushed her arms up and stretched, answering before Tyler could, "No, we don't have that luxury. We have to pick up the babies tonight. Our babysitter is leaving town in the morning."

"See, they are doing it," Carissa said.

"Yes, but we *have* to," Tyler said. "I'd rather just go to bed. I need a shower first. My beard is eighty percent sweat right now."

"What's the other twenty percent?" Loki asked.

"Mainly vomit and whiskey," Tyler smiled.

"Ew," Flea said as she threw a playful elbow into her husband's stomach. "Don't try and kiss me until that thing is washed."

Tyler leaned and mocked kissing; "Come on, babe. Just a smooch."

"No," Derek said. "That's not what you say."

"What?" Tyler turned to his friend.

"You have to say: *you get kissies*," Derek said with a french accent.

The group burst into laughter, at the reference to a joke from earlier on the trip. The kind of joke that every person knew that at some point they would try to explain to a co-worker or family member, but it would fall flat because it was a joke that landed safely in the "you had to be there" category. Still, the group laughed until their stomachs hurt.

The black van creeped down the lonely highway. The lights of the city started to peek out of the darkness. The only other vehicles on the road were semi-trucks; at two in the morning there weren't many cars out and about in the small town. The van drove past a truck stop, an abandoned mini-golf course, and a lumber mill, all of which were just check points in Derek's head that said to him that they were almost home.

"So," Carissa said as she turned around to Flea and Shawna, "you guys still want to get together Saturday? Do our little lunch thing?"

"Oh, yes," Shawna said, as she ran a brush through her hair, combing out the bed-head. "I forgot all about that."

"Me too," Flea admitted with a deep chuckle. "I forgot we even made lunch plans."

"Because you made them when you were all shit-ass-drunk," Thomas said. "You guys were already a full bottle of vodka in, before you guys climbed into the hot tub. I remember you guys squealing about brunch and everyone saying how great it sounds."

"That sounds about right," Carissa laughed and smiled. "I just woke up with a note written on my hand about lunch."

"You don't even remember the conversation?" Derek looked over at his wife, his face stern but playful.

Carissa smirked and shook her head.

"Disappointed," he said with a smile.

The van moved from the highway and onto the last stretch before they would arrive at Thomas and Shawna's house. Loki, Tyler and Flea had all met at their house and together they had gone and picked up Derek and Carissa.

"Hey, can I run in and use the bathroom really quick?" Loki asked. "I've seriously drank too much water back here. I feel like I'm about to piss myself."

"Please don't", Shawna said. "My kids sit back here."

"Your kids have sat in a pissy seat plenty of times," Loki joked.

"Yeah, but it's *their* piss. Not a grown ass-man's," Thomas said.

"Fine, then let me use your bathroom," Loki reiterated.

"If it stops you from pissing in my van you can piss in whatever room you please," Tyler said.

"Deal," Loki said.

"No, no, that's not a deal. Stop it," Shawna said. She pushed a finger out towards Loki and used her best *mom* voice. "No."

Loki raised his hands in the air, "Whoa, fine. I'll just piss in the toilet like a civilized human."

"Dude, I saw some of the stuff you did this weekend. You are anything *but* civilized," Derek said.

"I said *like*," Loki said. "I'll do my best impression."

Derek turned off the road and then took another turn into the driveway of the house.

"Fucking finally," he said to himself as he rubbed the bottom of his palms into his eye sockets.

Carissa reached up and pressed a couple buttons on the dash that opened both sliding doors and the back of the van. Everyone slowly climbed out of the van and did their own version of stretching out the kinks from the long drive home.

"Seriously," Loki said as his hands covered his crotch and he began to bounce.

Thomas looked over to his wife and then back to Loki, "You know the combo, go ahead."

Without answering, Loki turned from the group and walked towards the house.

"Hey, where did we put our keys?" Flea asked as she opened her purse and shuffled through it.

"You put them inside, remember?" Derek answered.

"Oh, that's right," Flea said. "Babe, could you get the bags out and I'll grab the keys?"

Tyler nodded before moving to the back of the van in search of their bags.

"I gotta pee too," Carissa said to her husband.

Derek looked at her and shrugged, "Well, then go." He pointed towards the house with a grin. "Before they tell you no."

Carissa kissed her husband on the cheek and sprinted after the girls.

"You've got packages!" Loki screamed from the door.

CHAPTER TWO

THIS ALL ENDS HORRIBLY | 12

Flea followed Shawna from the van into the front yard of her house. The motion light flicked off but almost immediately shot back to life when the two girls stepped out in front of it.

"Wait up," Carissa said as she jogged up to them. "Don't leave me with the guys."

Shawna chuckled and grabbed her friend's hand, "We would never want you to be in such a bad situation as that."

Flea smiled as they continued towards the door that Loki left open. In front of the doorway were a couple of boxes, neatly stacked together like rows on a tetris game.

"Did a little shopping while we were gone?" Flea asked.

"I think it was drunk-Shawna. She has a problem with Amazon and alcohol together," Shawna said as she leaned down and grabbed two boxes.

Carissa reached down and grabbed two more, leaving the last one for Flea to reach down and grab.

The box was so light, it almost felt empty. It didn't look like any Amazon box she had ever received. There was no address attached or any indication it was mailed. "This one is weird," she said to the girls as they stepped into the house.

"Let me see," Shawna said, as she put down her boxes on a circular coffee table in the front room then turned around with a hand out. Shawna inspected the box, flipping it around a couple times before lightly shaking it. "Oh, it *is* weird."

Flea looked down the hallway towards the bathroom, then looked up the staircase, a more pressing issue at hand. "Can I use your bathroom? I don't want to follow behind whatever Loki is doing down here."

Shawna nodded as she placed the small box on the table with the rest of them.

"Thanks," Flea said as she moved from the front room towards the staircase. The staircase went up six steps, before a landing turned it back and up in the opposite direction the rest of the way to the second floor. Flea looked at the pictures hung up on the wall. Pictures of Thomas and Shawna on their wedding day, Thomas shoving a large piece of cake into Shawna's mouth while she laughed and got cake on her white dress. Another framed picture of their family all sitting on the ground surrounded by a fall setting, the kids sitting on their parents' laps. More pictures that Flea had seen hundreds of times, until she stopped at the landing and saw a new one, a wood-burned frame that she wouldn't take as anything that Shawna would have purchased. The picture was of a dark forest at night. The house wasn't really decorated with anything other than family pictures. Shawna had been talking about getting some artwork to hang around the house, but Flea thought she was referring to paintings, or canvases with quotes, or something along those lines. This was weird and felt *off*. Shivers ran down Flea's spine as she forced her body to turn away from the scene and back towards her mission of using the upstairs bathroom.

At the top of the stairs there was a hallway that led to two bedrooms and a bathroom on the left, and another two bedrooms and the laundry room on the right. Flea turned towards the door that she knew was the master bedroom. She wasn't about to use the other bathroom, which was the kids' bathroom. It was a known fact that in this house, the kids were gross and so was that bathroom. Flea opened the door to her friends' bedroom.

She paused.

Flea knew something was different before she even flicked the light on. Even in the minimal light shining through the bedroom window from the moon, she could see that the room was empty. Flea reached in and flipped the lightswitch. The light juddered before finally turning on. The room was empty. The large bed and nightstands, the desk with Shawna's computer, the laundry basket, and even the mountain of clean clothes that Thomas and Shawna always neglected to fold were gone. Just a soft gray carpet that looked untouched remained. The walls were even bare. Flea couldn't recall what was usually on it, maybe a mirror and pictures? There might have been a bejeweled elephant head or something. Still, the walls had nothing of the sort now.

Flea took a step back and yelled down the stairs, "Shawna!"

Shawna popped her head around the staircase, "Sup?"

"You need to come up here," Flea said, "quick." Her voice was stern and flat.

She saw Shawna turn and talk to Carissa, before both girls walked up the staircase towards Flea. Shawna stopped at the same picture for a moment before turning back towards Flea.

"What's going on?" Shawna asked.

Flea pointed towards the open master bedroom.

Shawna stepped inside. "Oh my god."

Carissa poked her head in, "Oh fuck, you were robbed!"

Shawna walked around the empty room with her arms out, "Wh–whh–what? Why?"

"I'm sorry, friend," Carissa said as she placed a hand on Shawna's shoulder. "We should call the cops."

"Who would do this, seriously?" Shawna asked. "Why take *everything*? What do they want with pictures of Thomas and I? Why take our dirty clothes? This feels personal."

"Did you post any pictures of us while at Disneyland?" Carissa asked.

Flea stepped into the room. It felt strange. Like Shawna was moving out. She could even see what reminded her of vacuum lines through the carpet.

"Yeah, so?" Shawna queried.

"Well, that could have let people know you were out of town and think it was a good time to break in," Carissa said.

"Don't," Shawna said as she pointed towards her friend. "What the fuck am I going to do? They even took my work computer. I have to pay for that!"

"I'm sorry," Flea said.

"What do I do?" Shawna wailed.

Flea looked over to Carissa and shrugged.

A rush of cold air hit Flea like a wave. She felt it slide from the left side of her body to the right. The small hairs on her arms spiked like tiny daggers on her skin. Flea felt her hair move as if a gust of wind had hit her face.

Then the door slammed shut.

"Good god," Tyler said. "What is she doing in there?" He dropped the final bag beside the others in front of the car. The long trip required more bags than

Tyler wanted. He managed to fit everything he needed into a single travel bag; that wasn't the case with Flea however. Flea was a classic overpacker. A bag for casual clothes. A bag for shoes and sandals. A bag for fancier clothes, on the off chance the group went to a nice dinner (they didn't). A bag for makeup. And a final bag for underwear and a couple swimsuits, because she didn't know which one she was going to need on which day.

He wanted to complain about the amount of bags his wife needed, but knew he wouldn't get any sympathy. Flea wasn't the only girl who packed like she was leaving for a month; all of the girls did it… and Loki too. Loki probably had more bags than any individual girl in the group, although Tyler had absolutely no idea for what reason.

"You know the girls," Derek said. "They can't do anything alone. I'm sure all the girls are together in the bathroom, just talking."

"I'm exhausted, I want to get home," Tyler said.

Thomas closed the van door, "That's everything that needs out of here right now. All that's left is you two's stuff and our own." Thomas directed his statement towards Derek.

"Thanks," Derek responded.

Thomas stepped up with the two men, then he turned back towards the house. "Shit sure is taking a while."

"Right?" Tyler asked.

"Well, if we want to go to sleep before the sun rises, we better get 'em," Derek said.

"And maybe pry Loki from my bathroom before he makes himself at home and passes out on the toilet again," Thomas said as the group moved from the van towards the gate. The motion light flickered on before flickering back off.

"When did that happen?" Tyler asked. He looked up at the motion light; he remembered helping Thomas install it after their exterior cameras kept catching someone lingering in front of Thomas's house, a couple days in a row. It freaked Shawna out and she insisted on getting them. That was only a couple months ago, they shouldn't be acting up already. He made a mental note to check it out later, maybe next time they all got together for dinner.

"After Shawna's thirtieth birthday party. When everyone had drunk themselves into oblivion," Thomas said.

"The one where your wife had us all dress like Adam Sandler characters?" Derek asked.

"That would be the one," Thomas said. "I walked into the bathroom the next morning and found a man dressed like Little Nicky passed out on the toilet."

"That was a weird party." Tyler laughed as he thought about the fifteen or so people dressed like Happy Gilmore, the ten people dressed like Billy Madison, and the handful of people dressed like other characters.

Thomas walked up to the keypad and punched in the numbers: 0713. The mechanical lock opened with a small chime of a bell, and Thomas pushed the door open.

Immediately a smell flooded Tyler's nostrils. He reared back his head.

"The fuck is that smell?" Derek asked.

Thomas covered his nose, "I have no fucking idea."

The men stepped inside the house, "Did you leave something out by mistake when you left? Like... I don't know... something defrosting by accident?" Tyler asked.

"Maybe your fridge went out?" Derek wondered aloud.

Thomas rolled his eyes, "Kinda annoying that the girls didn't say something." He stepped towards the hallway that led into the kitchen.

Tyler followed, keeping a tight pinch on his nostrils. The smell was unbearable. Something had spoiled. It reminded Tyler of a time he left a ham out by mistake in the garage. He pulled it out of the freezer and placed it on a barstool while he was digging in the freezer for chicken nuggies. It was a couple days before he went back in the garage, and by then the summer heat had made the ham nothing but a spoiled mess. The smell lingered in the garage for weeks.

"What's that?" Derek asked. Tyler and Thomas stopped and turned towards their friend.

Derek was hunched over with his hands on his knees, looking at something on the small table at the end of the couch. "You buy this?"

Thomas reached down and grabbed what Derek was looking at. Tyler looked over his shoulder and saw what he was holding. A mason jar with green yellow liquid; the glass was fogged and looked old.

Tyler grabbed the jar and shook it, and through the murky liquid a small eyeball bobbed against the glass. "Gross," he said.

"The wife getting Halloween stuff out early?" Derek asked.

"I don't remember ever seeing that out during Halloween," Thomas said. He grabbed the jar from Tyler, placed it back down, and shrugged, "I need to pay more attention to our bank account."

The men all moved down the hallway towards the kitchen. The smell became thicker. Tyler's eyes began to burn as they got closer. The smell was impossible to keep out by simply pinching your nose. Tyler felt his stomach turn as the smell triggered something in his brain that said: EJECT.

The three men turned the corner and froze.

"What the fuck?" Tyler said.

CHAPTER *THREE*

THIS ALL ENDS HORRIBLY

Loki unrolled a generous amount of toilet paper and wiped.

He reached around behind the toilet and grabbed a bottle of air freshener, and puffed a few mists out before standing, pulling up his pants, and flushing.

He looked into the mirror and checked his teeth before washing his hands. Loki used his tongue to move the small lip piercing he had in the center of his bottom lip. It bounced up and down as he ran the warm water over his hands. Once finished, he turned to the empty towel ring. He rolled his eyes and flung his hands, trying to get any of the excess water from his hands before just wiping them off on his shirt.

Loki pulled up on the door handle.

It didn't open.

He tried again, but the door didn't budge. The handle went all the way up, and should release, but didn't. Loki tried to position his head so he could watch the handle's mechanisms move as he pulled up again. Nothing. He couldn't see why it wasn't working.

"Hey!" Loki yelled. "Hey! I think your doorknob is busted."

Loki waited for a reply; he knew the girls were right behind him, and as long as he had been in the bathroom he was fairly certain that at least Thomas had come in. Unless Thomas and Shawna had gone together to drop off Derek and Carissa. Seemed unlikely that they would leave him alone and unattended in their house. They would have at least told him.

Loki yelled again and waited to see if he could hear a reply.

Nothing.

Loki closed the lid to the toilet and sat down on top of it. He was going to have to wait it out.

He reached into his pockets and pulled out his phone. He would have to call them then.

"Huh," Loki said as he looked at the screen that indicated there was no service. Loki pressed the restart button and waited for it to turn off and back on.

Loki rolled his neck until he felt a satisfying *pop*.

The trip home from Southern California was exhausting. He was a larger man, he had been his entire life. He had a lot of fun while on the trip, but he sweated through every piece of clothing he had brought with him. The beach was cool. It was the first time he had ever seen the ocean. He didn't care for humidity though. Growing up in Arkansas he didn't have a need for a drivers license, so it was fairly high up on his priority list now that he had moved to Oregon. Since he didn't have his license, he didn't split any of the driving duties with everyone else. It made him feel like a child, but he would make sure that wouldn't be a problem the next time they all traveled together.

Loki thought about how different everything had been over the last few months since making the *big move*. Leaving everything behind to move into a small apartment in Klamath Falls, Oregon. He and Thomas had met online over a decade ago. They had both been interested in comic books; Thomas was an illustrator and Loki was a writer. Together they had collaborated on several smaller projects, but they were ready to make a bigger move. They had a couple ideas that they believed could break them into the industry, but they wanted to make it happen quicker. No more emails and long conversations on the phone. Loki moved to chase his dream with Thomas.

"Hello?" Loki asked.

He turned his ear towards the door. It sounded like something was just outside the door. Loki waited for another sound. He held his breath and closed his eyes. Something shuffled outside the door, and he heard soft steps on the wooden floor.

"Hey!" Loki screamed. "The doorknob is broken or something. I can't get out."

He waited a moment for a reply.

"Listen, I didn't break it." He said. "I know it sounds like something I would do. And I think it's a safe assumption most times to think that I did, but not this time. I don't think so, at least."

No response. However, as Loki brought his ear closer to the door he could hear something.

He concentrated on what the sound was. It was soft. Low.

Whispering.

"I can't hear you," Loki said. "Seriously, you know how I feel about tight places, and this bathroom isn't exactly big. Could you help, please?"

More whispering.

"I'm about to ram this door down, no joke. I am starting to get upset."

Loki leaned his ear towards the door and tried to calm his breathing so he could hear the whispers.

"I want to peel your skin off," a voice whispered.

Loki pulled his head away from the door.

The whispers continued, although now they felt like they followed him. The whispers seemed to be in his head, climbing though his ear canal and slipping into his brain.

"I want to cut your body into little pieces and hide you inside my walls," the whisper said. "I want to keep you awake and have you watch as I cut off each finger and toe. Peel your skin off your arms and chest with a potato peeler and then feed it to you. I want to—"

Loki pressed his hands to his ears, hoping to disrupt the voice.

Loki opened his eyes and watched the doorknob lift. He reached down and grabbed it again, holding it shut.

The person behind the door was strong. He could feel it inch closer and closer towards opening even as Loki put his entire weight into it.

"Fuck," Loki said.

***

"What was that?" Carissa said as the door slammed behind them.

The single light fixed to a fan in the center of the master bedroom began to flicker.

Carissa walked over to the two girls.

Flea looked up at the lights, "It kinda did this when I walked in here."

"This bad?" Shawna asked.

Flea shook her head no.

The three women watched the light flicker faster and faster. The light going dim, to overly bright, to nearly off; back and forth with no discernible pattern.

Eventually the four bulbs inside the fixture *popped* as thin glass exploded into the room like shrapnel from a grenade.

The room was cast in a shadow of darkness. The moonlight from outside the window was no longer present. It was as if there wasn't a window at all anymore.

Carissa waited for her eyes to focus in the darkness, eventually showing the shapes of the girls beside her.

"What is going on?" Flea asked.

Carissa shook her head, "What's it called... when too much power happens? Like from the electric company or whatever?"

"Power surge?" Shawna asked.

"I think so," Carissa said. "I think it was just a power surge."

"Could a power surge explode the bulbs like that?" Flea asked from behind Carissa.

Carissa turned around to Flea, she still couldn't really see her, but recognized the large fluffy shape of her curly hair. She turned back to the other two shapes that she first saw. Carissa took out her phone and opened the flashlight app, pointing it towards the shadows.

Shawna placed a hand over her eyes and turned her head. "Jesus, lower that thing."

Then Carissa's heart began to race.

She didn't lower the phone like Shawna had asked. She couldn't move at all. Her knees began to quiver and she could feel her eyes begin to water, as behind her friend she could see something. Even with the minimal light that was given off by the small app on her phone, she could see something peeking its head around the corner to the bathroom.

A pitch black head and shoulders with fingers that gripped the exterior of the door.

Shawna smacked the phone from Carissa's hand, "Seriously."

The shock of the smack brought her back to the moment, "Sorry, I-I thought I saw something."

Shawna turned around in the direction Carissa was still looking.

"You did," Flea said from behind her.

Carissa turned around to see her friend had lost all color. She was as pale as Carissa had ever seen her. Flea raised her hand and pointed in the same direction that Carissa had just seen the shape.

Carissa then watched as the black fingers gripping the doorframe slowly released, and pulled back into the darkness.

Just as Carissa's phone died.

***

The smell was no longer the biggest issue.

Derek covered his nose and turned his head.

Behind him he heard a vomiting sound, either Tyler or Thomas couldn't handle it anymore.

His eyes began to water as Derek started to feel his stomach twist, moments away from vomiting. Derek closed his eyes and tried to hold it back.

"What–why?" Thomas asked.

Derek turned to his friend and then back to the kitchen.

Hung throughout the kitchen on meat hooks were dead bodies.

Several dead bodies.

All naked, with the hook pierced through their chest, the silver tips shining off the kitchen light. Their skin looked aged and old, like they had been left in the sun for too long. The skin almost looked *crunchy*. Various shades of brown and black. Derek could see that the first few people on a hook had their hands tied behind their back and their ankles had been taped together. Their faces looked like they had died in a terrible amount of pain. The closest was an elderly lady, her mouth wide open; Derek could see her dentures had slipped from their usual position and had remained on the tongue of her open mouth. White maggots crawled in and out of her exposed chest. The one beside her was a middle aged man, his thinning hair laying over his screaming face. His dry and cracking skin exposed a sleeve of tattoos on his left arm, another faded tattoo on his chest and stomach. His ankles weren't tied together, but were sloppily chopped off. Below him was a lake of blood and his feet stood perfectly below his dangling body.

Behind them were more bodies that Derek didn't dare to take visual inventory of. In the kitchen he could see the sink filled to the brim with a black liquid that looked both chunky and slimy at the same time.

He saw there was another younger woman, she might have been a teenager. A small child, maybe ten years old or so. Another man. And the one that finally made Derek lose his lunch… A pregnant lady.

Below her hanging body was a pile of blood, shit, and guts. As Derek looked harder, he saw a small baby; face down inside the gross pile.

Derek leaned over and blew chunks across Thomas's dining room.

"I need to call someone," Thomas said as he backed away. "We need to get out of here and not contaminate anything."

Derek wiped his mouth and shook his head, "Agreed. We need to get the girls out of here too. And Loki, if he's still here." He felt whatever left in his body climb up again, before he forced it back down with a large swallow.

The men stepped backwards into the front room, "Girls!" Tyler screamed.

"We need you to come outside with us!" Thomas screamed.

They waited for a response.

Nothing.

"Girls!" Tyler screamed again.

Thomas leaned over to Derek, "I left my phone in the van, can I borrow yours?"

Derek pulled his out of his pocket, handing it to his friend.

"How are we gonna explain this?" Tyler asked.

Derek shrugged, "We don't have to, we've been gone. We have plenty of proof of that."

"Those bodies look like they've been there for *ages*," Tyler said.

"Well, they haven't," Thomas said as he took the phone from Derek and looked at the screen. "Your phone isn't dialing out."

"What does that mean?" Derek asked.

"I mean… I can't call out with it." Thomas said.

"Girls!" Tyler screamed again. "Fucking get down here! This is an emergency!" He threw on his best *dad* voice. A voice he still hadn't mastered with his own son, but he figured that would come with experience, he was still new to the "father game".

"Maybe they already went back to the van," Thomas said, as he walked over to the front door.

"Yeah, probably," Derek said.

As Thomas's hands slipped around the doorknob, he froze.

Derek heard it.

He knew why Thomas had stopped.

From inside the kitchen, he heard a sound.

A baby crying.

CHAPTER FOUR

THIS ALL ENDS HORRIBLY | 28

Loki couldn't hold the doorknob anymore.

He could feel the sweat on his hands making them slip.

"Please," Loki grunted, "stop."

Loki gritted his teeth and put everything he had left into the doorknob.

The voice behind the door whispered again, "I'm going to pull your lungs out through your mouth."

Then the handle was released.

Loki fell to the floor, not letting go of the handle, but also well aware that he wasn't really doing much in stopping anyone from opening it. He had exerted every ounce of energy he had to keep whoever it was out.

He double checked that he had locked the door and reached for the hand towel, belatedly remembering that the towel rack was empty. Again, he used his shirt to wipe the sweat. Loki looked up at the mirror and breathed in deep. He felt an emotion climb down and latch itself to the core of his body. Like a parasite attaching itself to a host. *Fear.* Loki began to cry. Tears flooded from his eyes as he began to have a hard time catching his breath. He hyperventilated and gasped for air as his vision was obstructed by the water streaming from his eyes. "What the actual fuck," Loki said to himself.

Loki didn't stop it. He let the emotion overrun his entire body. He fell to the floor of the small bathroom and tucked his legs up to his chest and cried. He had no idea what had just happened, but he was glad it was over. Loki felt his chest heave up and down as he slowly began to regain control of his breathing, which slowly brought him back to the situation at hand.

Loki rolled over and reached into his pocket, pulling out his phone.

With all the events that had just transpired, he didn't even notice that the phone had reset and turned back on.

Bing.

Bing.

Bing-bing.

Bing-bing-bing.

Loki almost dropped the phone as his fingertips struggled to open the lock screen. Eventually, he was able to enter his passcode. At the bottom of the homescreen was the message icon with a red bubble that told him he had seven unread messages. Loki opened the app, and to his surprise, the messages were from his own phone number. He hesitantly opened the unread thread. Seven images appeared on the screen. Pictures of himself. Loki looked up from his phone and then back to the images; they looked as if they were taken from the mirror. In the photos, Loki sat on the toilet.

Loki got to the final photo. How was this happening? He looked up at the mirror, it wasn't a two-sided mirror. He had been there when Shawna had bought it refurbished before hanging it in the small bathroom. Loki looked down at the picture again, scrolling from the beginning to the end.

Something in the second picture caught his attention. Something that was over his shoulder. A black figure that was out of focus. Loki scrolled to the next picture, it was a little more visible now, yet still mainly hidden behind his shoulder. He scrolled and scrolled, watching as the black figure slowly came into view. In the final of the series of photos, he saw a black hand, fully formed planted on his shoulder.

His heart felt like it stopped beating as he noticed movement in the corner of his eye. Something over his shoulder.

Loki looked up at the mirror in front of him. In the reflection he saw a shadow of a hand sitting on his shoulder.

Then the light turned off and he was swallowed in the dark.

***

"What the *fuck* is that?" Shawna asked as she fumbled in her own pockets, trying to recover her phone.

"It was a person!" Flea screamed. "Someone is in here!"

Shawna heard the footsteps of her friends moving towards the back corner of the empty bedroom.

Finally, she recovered her phone and slipped it from her pocket. She pressed the button on the side, but it was of no use. Her phone was also dead.

"Flea," Shawna said, "try your phone."

Shawna heard Flea pat around her pockets, but she never took her gaze off the general direction of the bathroom. Sure, it was pitch dark, but she knew in which direction she had seen the figure.

"I–I don't have it," Flea said. "I think I left it in the car."

"We need to get out of here," Carissa said.

Shawna reached her hands out and felt around for her two friends. She found them and then crawled her hands down their arms until she had a friend's hand in each of her own. She locked her fingers tight around theirs. "Okay, we can just all move together. Don't let go. We will slowly move towards the door."

Before anyone could take a step forward, an orange glow burst through the large window beside them. All of a sudden the entire room was covered in light. It wasn't a steady light; it wavered incredibly fast, but still, they could see the room now. The bathroom doorway where they had seen the hand slip into the darkness was now closed. They didn't hear the door close, but the bathroom door was nonetheless shut.

"Do you hear that?" Carissa asked.

Shawna listened.

"It sounds like something is... *crackling*," Carissa answered her own question.

Shawna felt Carissa pull her arm as she moved to the window. Together all three women moved as one and witnessed where the orange glow came from. The large tree that was in the center of Shawna and Thomas's backyard was now on fire. The horizon outside was washed in red like a large harvest moon. The flames from the tree rippled through the air; air also thick with plumes of smoke. The heat of the flames were hot enough to be felt on Shawna's face.

She opened her mouth to say something, but nothing came out. There were a million questions to ask, although no one in the room had any of the answers.

The view through the window looked like it was as though the end of the world was happening. Trails of smoke rose in the distance, as neighborhoods appeared as if they were on fire. Ash fell from the sky like snowflakes stuck in a winter flurry. Shawna focused her eyes on the road beside the house. She saw someone walk out from one of the houses and lay in the center lane of the three-lane road. Another person walked out of the same house, holding the hands of a smaller person, most likely a child. Across the street, two people walked out. Shawna had known this couple, seeing how they shared a back fence. They were an elderly couple, Marabeth and Richard. They would always bring a small gift for their children each Christmas. Marabeth and Richard walked to the center lane and stood side-by-side with the other people. Then, almost in unison, each person moved together to their knees, laying their foreheads down on the street's asphalt.

"What are they doing?" Flea asked.

Shawna realized that all three of them were zoned into the same thing. Not only that, but she realized that she couldn't look away. Shawna tried to turn her head to look at Flea or Carissa, but couldn't. Her head was locked in and her eyes were unmoving.

Then, from the furthest point from the window, a man with a limp walked out towards the group in the road. He carried a red jug that immediately made Shawna's breathing race. She knew what the jug was. It was a generic jug that most people kept inside their shed or garage.

"Is that a gas can?" Carissa asked.

No one answered her as the man limped over to the line of people with their heads on the ground, and watched as he slowly poured out the bottle on each person before dumping the rest on his own body, and laying down at the front of the row. The man sat up and looked up at the window, toward the girls watching. He stared without movement; his eyes burning hotter than the flames from the tree. Eventually, he slowly moved a hand to his pocket and retrieved a small lighter.

"Don't," Shawna whispered.

He flicked the lighter a couple of times before the flame exploded from it. There was barely a moment to understand what was happening as the small flame expanded rapidly down the man's arm and across his body. He layed back down fully as the flame sprinted from him to the person beside him, and then one by one down the line. Shawna watched as the flames ate their clothing and charred their flesh. Their skin turned black as the flames ripped them open and oozes of puss leaked from the wounds. The smell of the burning flesh wafted through the air and penetrated the closed window. Shawna could smell the burnt hair and skin mixed with the smell of charred clothing and the burnt rubber of shoes.

Shawna fought to turn her gaze. To look at anything else besides this scene. She pulled as hard as she could, and slowly she was able to inch her head away from her neighbors on fire on the ground below. Shawna kept turning her head until she was looking at her own reflection in the window.

Behind her she watched as the bathroom door slowly opened.

All of a sudden everything disappeared. She watched as the flames sucked back into the tree. The charred and black smoke of her neighbors' bodies paused, and then with a blink of an eye, they were gone.

The girls were standing in front of the window, looking out into the darkness of a long summer night. Shawna could barely make out the outline of the tree, but she was still able to faintly see it.

Carissa raised her hand and placed it on the window.

"It's still warm," she said.

Shawna raised a hand and touched the glass. "You're right."

"So, that wasn't in our head?" Flea asked.

"I–I don't know," Shawna admitted.

"Come on, let's get ou—" Carissa started before coming to an abrupt stop.

Shawna felt her arm whip in the air as she felt Carissa's hand pull her own, still gripped together from their first attempt to leave the room.

The suddenness of it, and the strength of it, meant that Shawna felt one of her best friends slip from her fingers with little ability to stop it.

All she heard in that moment was Carissa's screams as she was ripped into the darkness, into the direction of the bathroom.

***

Tyler watched as Thomas released the door knob and turned back to the other two men.

Tyler heard it. He didn't want to hear it, but he did.

"Was that–" Thomas began.

"Sure was," Derek cut him off.

The men stood quietly at the door for a moment longer.

"Do we check it out?" Thomas asked.

Tyler looked over to Derek, trying to read his face. Derek looked from Thomas to Tyler, then back to Thomas. His face was flat. Derek shrugged, "I feel like we have to, right?"

"I would argue that we don't," Tyler said with a finger in the air. "We make the call, then worry about the baby."

"You just don't want to go back in there," Thomas said.

"Fucking right I don't!" Tyler exclaimed. "Did you see the same thing as me? Blood. Guts. Shit. Everywhere. No, I don't want to go back inside the kitchen! I don't think any of us do."

"I'll go then," Derek said.

"Really?" Thomas asked.

"Yeah," Derek said. "Just wait for me. Okay?"

"No," Tyler said as he reached out a hand to stop his friend from moving. "Stop. We will all go. I'm not gonna let you walk in there alone."

Derek nodded his head. Tyler could see relief wash over his friend's face. He didn't want to go alone, but he would have, if he needed to. Tyler wasn't excited about going back inside there either, but knew that he would never forgive himself if something happened to Derek alone in there.

Together the men walked back to the kitchen.

The footsteps were short and soft. They were no longer walking around Thomas's house, they were walking through someplace evil. Someplace that had been birthed from the anus of hell and shit out in the middle of their friends' kitchen.

Derek peeked his head around the corner and into the room. He hesitated then stepped fully into the room. "The fuck?"

Tyler and Thomas followed.

The room was bare.

Exactly as Thomas had left it.

The kitchen floor was once again clean and shiny. No dead bodies hung from the ceiling. The sink was empty and clean. It was exactly as Tyler had last seen it before they left for the trip.

"And that would be our cue to leave," Tyler said as he turned back towards the front door.

"Sure as fuck is," Tyler said as Thomas raced around him. Tyler followed.

***

Thomas was at the front door. He had moved from the kitchen to the front door in only a few seconds, but it felt like it had taken forever. The trauma of seeing the room covered in horror had his heart already racing, but the reveal of the room being normal again had it pick up another notch. Sure, it was better, but now Thomas couldn't explain what had happened. Before, it was easy to explain that some psycho had broken into the house while they were gone. Killed people and made a horror-show in the kitchen, then left before getting caught. Now?—now it wasn't as easy to explain. Thomas didn't believe in the paranormal, but he sure knew when something didn't feel right.

He reached his hand around the handle and twisted.

Thomas felt something on the top of his head.

He turned around and looked over at his friends.

Their eyes locked in on Thomas's head. Wide. Terrified.

Then Thomas felt *pressure*.

Pressure, and a sharp pain around his forehead.

His vision was obscured.

He felt a warm liquid running down his face and slip into his mouth.

Thomas tasted nickel.

He screamed as he brought his hands up to his head, and felt his skin peeling back slowly...

CHAPTER *FIVE*

THIS ALL ENDS HORRIBLY | 36

Loki pounced from the closed toilet to throw himself against the wall beside him. He heard the crunch of the drywall as he slammed his large body against it violently.

In the darkness of the small bathroom, Loki felt his knee bang against the sink, sending a sharp pain shooting up his knee.

He fell to the ground and reached for his shoulder, hoping to knock whatever was on his shoulder off.

He rolled to his back and tried to slowly regain his breathing. Back and forth. Feeling his chest rise and fall. He was spread out along the bathroom floor, the cold tile beneath his bare skin clammy on his neck and arms.

Before he could fully catch his breath though, the light shot on.

Loki tried to cover his eyes above his face, but couldn't move. He looked down to see his arms strapped beside him.

Even worse, he was no longer on the bathroom floor. He was on a table. The kitchen table in the dining room, in fact. His arms were pulled tightly on each side of him and tied down below. His feet were also restrained, leaving his legs spread slightly.

Loki looked around the room, searching for anything he could use to free himself.

The dining room was not as Loki had remembered it.

The few framed pictures in the room were covered with a white sheet. The rest of the furniture was stacked in the corner of the room, and the large cabinet that held Shawna's fancy dishes was also covered in a white sheet.

Loki tried to release his hands, but the more he tried, the more he could feel the rope tightening around them.

He heard footsteps behind him. Someone was walking slowly, but with a heavy step. It sounded like it was back in the kitchen, far enough away that Loki knew he still had time to escape.

None of this made sense.

Not anything from what happened in the bathroom, to being locked in with the voice and the hand, to being teleported to this table, made any sense.

He needed to escape. Get out and make a run for the back door. Whoever was coming after him was in no hurry to get there, surely he still had time.

Loki bit down and pulled with both arms. He had always prided himself on his strength; a man of his size always had a little more in the tank than most. The rope burned and pinched his skin as he pulled.

The footsteps he heard behind him suddenly stopped. Loki held his breath and waited for whatever would happen next. Waited for what felt like an eternity.

He could feel his chest rise and fall, over and over. The room started to feel smaller, as if the walls were falling in towards him.

Loki leaned his head back, hoping to see what it was that had approached him.

He looked back and saw a familiar face looking back at him.

"Arial?" He asked.

Arial smiled back at him. Not in the way he was used to. Not the way she smiled towards him back in Arkansas, the last place he had seen her. She was the only girlfriend that Loki had ever considered marrying. She was enough to keep him grounded. Settle down. Get a job that clocked in at seven in the morning, and allowed him to walk out the door at four in the afternoon. She was funny and smart. Loki had spent the better part of his adult life with her. Every "grown up" memory he had, she was present in. First drink of alcohol, she was there. The first time smoking weed, she was there. The first sale of his script to an indie comic book publisher, she was there, with a cake and a smile. Arial was more supportive of him than anyone had ever been. It was not having her anymore that really made Loki leave his home state, to travel across the country and start over.

Her death was just too much for him.

And yet she stood right beside him, but with a different smile than she had given to him every night before they laid down to sleep.

She wore the same blue dress that her family had buried her in, only now it looked faded and falling apart. Her hair was pulled up in a ponytail, revealing the wound on her head from the car crash that had taken her life so suddenly. Sure, the mortician had done his best job at covering it with makeup the day of the wake, but clearly it didn't last the year or so she had been beneath the earth. The crack in her skull looked infected, pusy. Green goo slipped from the creases in her scalp and down her forehead.

"Hey, baby," she said back. Her voice was crackly and harsh. As if in their time apart she had picked up chain-smoking cigarettes, and instead of exhaling, she just kept it all packed tightly in her lungs. "I missed you."

Loki yanked his arms, hoping to find a way loose. "Yeah, me too. I see–you — I mean, you look just lovely."

Arial smiled, "Aw–shucks– thanks, baby."

"Don't mention it," Loki said as he pulled his right arm with all of his might. There was no use trying to hide it; Arial clearly didn't care that he was trying to get out.

She reached a hand out and placed it on Loki's forehead, brushing his hair to the side of his face. Arial leaned down and kissed it. Her dry lips felt like sandpaper on his skin. Arial then lowered her body below the table and out of Loki's sight.

"You know," Loki said as he continued to wriggle, "I'm thinking, now that you're back... maybe we could pick up where we left off?"

He paused and waited for a response.

"Maybe move back into my little dinky apartment. You'd love it here. Oregon is like Arkansas, only no sales tax and the hicks here don't generally have flaming crosses. You have to get used to the winter though. I am working on my winter weight, if you know what I mean."

Slowly Arial rose from beneath the table, carrying a small wooden crate. She slammed it down on the dining table with a thud. "That would be *lovely*."

"Great, great, great," Loki trailed off as he tried to wrench his neck to peek inside the crate. "So maybe, I don't know, cut me loose. We can get going?"

Arial's smile slowly dropped into a frown, "I wanted to play a game first." She slowly lowered a hand into the crate.

"I–Yeah, I don't think I'm in the mood for games. Long trip home. I'm exhausted. I went to take a shit and then was harrassed by..."

Arial smiled again.

"You? It was you outside the door," Loki said.

Arial laughed. The same cute laugh that made Loki's heart swoon all those years ago. It was young and innocent. She nodded.

"Ah, okay, kinda rude," Loki said.

Arial lifted a hand from the box and revealed an item. Loki tried to focus on what she was holding, but in the darkness it just appeared as an indeterminate shape, no bigger than a couple of inches with the handle.

"Oh, I'm sorry," Arial said as she leaned the item closer for him to investigate.

A handheld potato peeler. The same kind Loki knew they had back home in Arkansas. The black handle with a silver blade, attached to fixed metal.

"What's, uh, the plan here, sweetie?" Loki asked.

Arial moved her free hand down Loki's chest as if they were legs marching down a trail, one finger lifting before coming back down, and the other following the pattern. She moved her fingers down his chest and towards his legs. They continued marching as Arial repositioned herself, moving down the table. The fingers stopped at his calf, at his tattoo.

"This is new," she said.

"Yeah," Loki confirmed. "Got it... you know, afterwards."

A single fingernail traced the outline of the tattoo. The sunflower, her favorite flower, with *Arial* written in script over the top. "I don't like it."

"Oh," Loki said. "Kind of a bummer to hear that, but hey, that's what a cover-up is for."

Arial continued to trace the tattoo with her fingertip, "No, I've got a better plan." She raised the potato peeler above her head so Loki could see it.

Loki's eyes grew wide as he took in the sight. He began to squirm again.

"Nawp," he said. "That sounds like a bad idea. One of your worst."

Arial laughed again, only this time it didn't feel like the same innocent laughter he had always loved. It felt playful yet menacing. "Hold still, I wouldn't want to go too deep."

Loki felt the blade of the peeler press against his calf; the cold steel sending shivers down his spine. Sweat streamed down his face as he shook his head.

"This is going to sting," Arial said.

***

"Carissa!" Flea screamed as she watched her friend disappear in the shadows of the bathroom.

Flea stepped forward, only to be stopped by Shawna.

"Wait," Shawna whispered with a finger pressed to her lips.

Flea took a moment to register the situation. She had just watched one of her best friends being ripped away into the darkness, after witnessing a horror scene unfold outside the window. The empty bedroom was still swallowed by shadows and now she was being told to *wait*. Wait for what? Things were going from zero to a hundred every second that passed, and Flea felt no urge to wait and see what happened next. She pushed Shawna out of her way and stepped forward.

The light in the center of the room flickered.

It startled Flea and she hesitated, then slowly inched forward. The abrupt change from pitch black to the flickering of the light felt like she was standing in the middle of a rave, and a strobe light was set to "PANIC".

Then Flea saw it.

In only the corner of her eye at first, she saw something. She wasn't sure what though. Yet between the flashes, as the light was momentarily on, she saw *something* in the corner of the room.

Flea paused and focused.

Every time the light flickered on and off with a numbingly loud hum, it seemed to penetrate Flea's ears and stick into her brain like a maggot on raw meat. There was a shape in the corner. As the light picked up, Flea took a step forward, her shoe crushing glass beneath her feet.

"Oh shit," Flea whispered to herself, as she lifted the shoe from the ground to see the small shards of glass from the lightbulb that had *popped* only moments ago. She looked up to the flickering light in the center of the room to see there was no actual bulb. The shining light was a small globe in the center of the room, not from the light fixture or a flashlight, but just floating. A feeling washed over

Flea as she looked into the light. She felt warm. Safe. At ease. In that moment she forgot what she was panicking about in the first place. What was so important only seconds ago? She smiled and took a step closer.

Behind her she could hear Shawna. She was saying something, but Flea couldn't muster up enough energy to care. All that mattered was the light. She chuckled to herself when her brain fixated on the idea of a moth to a flame. She understood what was so appealing for that moth in that moment. The calling of the glow. The energy the light gave off made her heart race, but not as it was earlier. She wasn't scared; she was excited. Excited to be consumed by the light. To feel it wrapped around her and keep her safe.

Again she heard Shawna behind her.

***

Derek saw it happen.

Watched thin black fingers wrap around Thomas's face on each side. They crawled across his face like spiders on a web. The fingers dug into the space between Thomas's eye sockets and pinched the skin around it. It pulled back, and Derek watched as Thomas's skin was removed from around his skull. Like a hoodie on the back of a sweatshirt, it was pulled back in one bloody movement. Thomas screamed for a second, but it happened fast enough that the scream stopped almost immediately. Even across the room, Derek felt the splash of warm blood splatter against his own face, and he wiped it away to see his other friend standing at the door.

Thomas raised his hands to his face and felt the exposed muscle and flesh. Blood ran down his hands as he carefully touched it.

"I–I– I can't feel anything," Thomas said as he started to fall to the ground.

Tyler reached down and grabbed him before he completely collapsed.

Derek sprang to his friend's side and helped Tyler lower him to the ground.

Thomas's face was covered in blood. From his eye sockets, straight across the bridge of his nose, and up and over his scalp, the skin was all peeled back. His wide eyes looked from Derek to Tyler, panicked and scared.

"I can't feel it," Thomas said softly. "I can't feel my face."

"It's going to be okay," Tyler said. "That's just shock."

Derek looked down as the pool of blood started to grow beneath Thomas's head. He was losing blood quickly.

"I'm–I'm scared," Thomas said.

"Thomas, just hang on," Derek begged, as he stood up and approached the door. He grabbed the handle and began to twist it. Derek paused.

He looked back at his friends.

"Go! Fucking go get some help!" Tyler screamed.

Somehow, Tyler didn't feel the small black fingers crawling against his own face. Derek saw that from the shadows, a hand had crawled onto his face; just like what he had witnessed on Thomas's face only moments ago.

Derek released the doorknob.

"Something doesn't want us to go," Derek whispered.

He knelt down beside his friend.

"I don't understand," Tyler said.

"Me neither," Derek replied, as he watched the fingers crawl off Tyler's face and back into the shadows. "But I don't think we are leaving just yet."

"*Uhhh Uh.*"

Derek looked down at Thomas and watched as blood began to seep from his lips. Thomas coughed and splattered blood from his mouth; his body shook as he gasped.

"He's choking," Tyler said.

"Help me," Derek said as he grabbed Thomas by the shoulder and rolled him to his side. Derek began to pat him on his back as more and more blood drizzled from his mouth.

Thomas shook in spastic sprints for a moment more before his body was limp.

"Did he… did he…" Derek asked.

Tyler softly rolled Thomas over onto his back, "Yeah. He's gone."

Derek looked at his friend; someone he had known most of his life. His eyes were wide, as blood slid down his face. No eyelids to cover his eyes, just a blanket of blood.

And in the background, between the sobs of the men beginning to cry for their fallen friend, a baby began to scream.

CHAPTER SIX

THIS ALL ENDS HORRIBLY | 46

Loki felt the peeler slide against his calf. The blade snagged his white skin and sliced it with little effort. A shock of pain ran through Loki's body as he felt the peeler slowly slip down his leg. He could hear the blade slicing a strip of skin from it. He could hear it cutting through the leg hair. He could hear his heart beating through his chest. A warm sensation began to arrive. He wasn't sure if it was the shock of the attack on his calf, or if it was the blood finally running down his leg. It didn't matter either way, Arial had moved down the limb slowly and carefully.

"There," she said as she placed the peeler on the table. With her other hand she picked up the long strip of flesh and dangled it in front of Loki's face. "Isn't that nice."

Loki tried to not look, but regardless, he did. A fleshy ribbon of at least six inches long waved in his face. Blood fell from the skin and the white strip had only part of the tattoo centered.

"No more," Loki said. "You don't have to do more."

Arial chuckled, "No, I don't *have* to." She carefully placed the piece of flesh on the table and picked up the peeler. "But I really love the way you squirmed." A smile slipped over her face.

Loki closed his eyes and wrapped his hands around the straps holding him in place. He held on as hard as he could as he felt the cold blade placed against his leg once more.

Arial looked up at him again, the scar on her forehead dripping green goo that slid down her face and off her chin, landing somewhere on Loki's leg. "You ready?"

Loki didn't answer. He gripped the strap harder and waited for the assault. If she was enjoying his pain, he was going to do his best to not give her any pleasure. He would hide as much as he could, but knew he could only hold out for so long. He felt the blade slip down his leg, slowly and methodically. He could feel the metal slice between the skin and the meat of his calf. He could once again hear the kitchen gadget separate the two, the sound bouncing off the walls like a cannon going off in his ear. He held his breath and gripped down tighter. The tool didn't stop. It slipped further and further down his leg. Loki felt the warm sensation of blood shooting from the exposed wound; in the corner of his eye he saw a red squirt of blood shoot into the air.

Arial laughed and looked back at Loki.

A splash of blood was spread across her face, "You squirted!"

She chuckled and then looked back down.

Still, Loki didn't give her what she wanted. He didn't fight. He didn't squirm or scream. He gritted his teeth and held as still as possible. The pain continued to unfold in his leg. Loki could feel the cold metal utensil slide until it finished abruptly. Arial held up another fleshy ribbon and laughed, as blood spilled from the patch of flesh.

"Oh, you don't look like you are having any fun, hun," Arial teased, as her smile turned into a forced frown. The blood spreading across her face was more than just a splash now. There were streaks of red covering her white and decaying face, mixing with the pus and goo from her head trauma. She ran a finger across her brow, cleaning a stripe of blood and ooze from her forehead. She took the finger and placed it in her mouth, sucking the liquid from under her long fingernails. "I want you to have fun. Let's see what I can do."

She licked her lips, cleaning any of the blood and pus that had been smeared around them. Her tongue was black and stiff, with thick slime inside her mouth clinging to her lips and tongue, like the trail of a snail. "Don't you miss this, baby?" She placed her finger in her mouth again and moaned. "Don't you?"

Loki looked away towards the ceiling. In his peripheral he watched as she fixed her ponytail and ducked out of his view.

His heart began to pick up. His breathing matched the rhythm of his heart. Loki didn't know what to expect, as he felt the stiff, dead hand of his old love grip his inner thigh. She squeezed as she crawled her hand up his leg, her long and sharp nails digging into his skin and poking through the flesh. Her hands crawled closer and closer towards his crotch.

Loki tried not to move. He didn't want to give her a reaction.

Then something happened that he wasn't prepared for. A pain shot across his body like an electric shock. He forgot his goal of staying strong and immediately began to scream. He could feel Arial's lips pressed against his bloody calf, sucking against the exposed wound. Her stiff tongue licking and rubbing the raw meat like a pumice stone. She moaned and moaned as her hand gripped tighter and tighter on his thigh. Loki could feel the blood in his calf explode out as she continued to lick and suck it.

And Loki felt every second of it.

Arial looked up and smiled at him, blood smeared across her face as she rolled her stiff tongue and licked her lips clean. She squeezed tight against his thigh, the nails making a *pop* sound as they punctured the skin and dug into her leg.

"Ready?" She asked.

Loki didn't answer.

Arial lowered her head back towards his open wound.

Loki closed his eyes and gritted his teeth as he felt her stiff tongue slip into his bloody calf again.

***

Tyler tried to not look back at the lifeless body of his friend on the ground at the front door. His face was peeled off and nowhere to be seen. Just a pool of blood remained, over exposed muscle and meat. His eyeballs were wide and staring blankly up to the ceiling.

He tried his best to shake it off and focus on what they were trying to do.

Find that god-damn baby.

The crying was louder now.

It was all Tyler could hear.

He didn't want to enter the kitchen again; it was the last place he wanted to be, but something told him it wasn't going to stop. Nothing was going to stop.

They slowly peered around the corner and into the kitchen, unsure of what to expect.

The kitchen was once again just as Thomas and Shawna had left it.

No corpses.

No blood.

No guts.

Just freshly cleaned countertops, swept floors, and an empty sink.

"Well," Derek said, "I guess between the two, this would be the one I preferred."

Tyler nodded, "So then where is that fucking baby?"

Derek shrugged, "Maybe it's not a real baby?"

"What else would it be?"

"Something drawing us in, keeping us from escaping," Derek said. "Maybe it's nothing."

"Maybe," Tyler agreed.

The men stood still at the edge of the kitchen, waiting for something to happen. Listening for anything. Yet the house stood silent.

A small red light blinked at the far end of the kitchen.

"Derek?" Tyler whispered as he pointed at the light.

Derek looked at it and then back to Tyler, "I think that's their security camera. Thomas and Shawna leave them on when they go out of town."

"Maybe we should check them?" Tyler suggested.

Derek nodded his head, "Yeah. How?"

"Thomas didn't have his phone on him, did he?" Tyler asked.

"I don't think so," Derek confirmed. "We need to check." He looked back in the direction of the front door. "We need to go back."

Tyler thought about it for a moment before agreeing with his friend. He didn't want to go back. Didn't want to see the bloody remains of his friend, but knew they needed to get back to check the camera footage.

There was movement as something passed by the red, blinking light, in the back of the room. Something had walked past it. Tyler jumped back and automatically felt around for the light switch. His fingers fumbled against the wall, until finding the plastic plate, he flipped the switch on.

The kitchen was flooded with the soft glow of white, casting the light down the kitchen and partially to the room beyond. The next room was only slightly visible from this end of the kitchen, and whatever it was that passed in front of the light had gone into that room.

"You saw it too?" Derek whispered.

"Yeah," Tyler answered softly.

And then the silence was broken.

The soft cry of a baby slowly started at the far end of the room, before a small child began to crawl into their vision.

A baby, wearing only a diaper, crawled out and stopped. It opened its mouth and let out the most pathetic cry Tyler had ever heard.

"Fuck that baby," Tyler said.

"Come on," Derek said.

"Wait," Tyler said. "Something feels wrong."

"What do you mean?" Derek asked.

"I mean," Tyler thought about it. "We don't actually think this is a *real baby*, do we?"

Derek looked down the kitchen and then back to his friend. "Looks real."

"I mean, the corpses did too," Tyler pointed out. "And those literally disappeared."

"So what are you saying? We leave the baby?" Derek asked.

"It's not real," Tyler said. "I'm positive."

"It's a trap?" Derek asked.

"Fuck that baby."

"Yeah, fuck that baby."

Tyler went to turn, but again, something in the shadows caught his attention. A figure walked out slowly, a female. She slowly walked up to the baby, who was crawling down the long kitchen towards the men. The baby's face was red with exhaustion from screaming. Its chubby cheeks were swollen and puffy.

The female got to the baby and paused, then she slowly looked up to the men and smiled. A long smile that stretched across her face; stretched too far for Tyler to feel comfortable with.

"We are sure that's not a real baby, right?" Derek asked.

Tyler, at that moment, was less than sure. He felt a pressure on his chest that wasn't there moments ago, when he was ready to walk away from the screaming baby. Now, with the sinister smile on the face of the woman, he felt like he needed to protect the child for some reason.

"I don–" Tyler tried to say as the female used one leg to kick the baby from the crawling position to the ground.

Before Tyler could finish his sentence, the female raised her foot above the crying child's head.

"Tyler?" Derek said quietly.

Tyler grabbed Derek by the shoulder and moved him away from the kitchen entrance, and out towards the front room.

As they walked Tyler could hear the unmistakable sound of a foot *thudding* against the head of the infant. An audible wet sound followed by squishing, and a skull cracking against the floor. The crying stopped instantly, but the stomping didn't.

***

"Flea!" Shawna screamed as she watched her friend walk towards the light in the center of the room.

She reached out to stop her, grabbing her by the shoulder; but it was of no use. Flea continued forward, towards the light. Shawna covered her eyes as the strobing of it continued at a faster pace.

"Flea! Look away!" Shawna screamed.

The figure in the corner of the room moved.

With each flash of the light it had moved slightly forward, towards Flea.

Shawna watched in horror as it moved slowly across the room towards her friend, who had reached the light and stopped. Her face nearly touched the strobing light that had clearly pulled her into it.

As the figure moved closer and closer, Shawna tried to weigh her options. Her mind raced but it always returned to the same result: nothing good was about to happen. Carissa had still been dragged away into the bathroom. Flea was still in some kind of trance. The men clearly had no idea what was happening, and were probably doomed to look for the girls, winding up in the same situation. Shawna was all alone, but she didn't have to be.

Shawna screamed again, "Please! Flea! Please wake up!". She slowly took a single step towards the door, "Please! Don't make me do this!"

Another step.

A tear rolled down her cheek as she screamed for her friend to come back to her. The ghastly figure had moved halfway across the room, it was now almost at Flea. Shawna took a few more steps; she was almost to the door. Now her eyes were overwhelmed with tears as they flooded down her face. She wiped away as many as she could as she reached forward, towards the doorknob.

Then the strobing light stopped.

The room was swallowed by the darkness again.

Shawna reached out for the doorknob, but the tears on her hand made it hard for her to grip the round handle.

CRUNCH!

The sound of broken glass being stepped on came from the center of the room.

CRUNCH! CRUNCH!

The footsteps were moving towards her.

Shawna panicked, gripping the handle with both hands as she tried to open the door, however, it wasn't just her lack of grip that was the problem. It was refusing to open. It was as if someone was holding the doorknob from the other side and pulling it closed on her.

Shawna cried and screamed as she struggled to open the door.

The crunching sound stopped.

There was an unsettling silence in the room, only broken by the sound of the jiggling doorknob. Shawna pulled and pulled, trying to pry it open.

Then the sound of heavy feet against the floor broke out in a full sprint towards her.

THUD THUD THUD THUD THUD!

Shawna let out a scream as every ounce of oxygen escaped her lungs. She pulled the door open, and just as the heavy steps reached her, she leapt forward and slammed the door closed behind her.

THUMP!

The door shook with the impact of something slamming against it.

Shawna fell to the floor, back pressed against the door, and lost it. She lost control, and the tears streamed down her face. Her breathing became rapid and hard. She felt dizzy; lightheaded to the point that she was afraid she was about to pass out.

However, she couldn't. She needed to get outside and find the guys. Tell them what was happening. Call... whoever you *can* call with whatever was happening! The cops? 911? A priest? A whole fucking clergy?

Shawna tried to regain her composure, failing, but at least she could stand up and move forward.

She walked to the railing of the stairs and looked down. Her heart picked up again, only now with excitement as she saw Derek and Tyler below the staircase, heading towards the front door.

"G-G-Guys!" She screamed through the tears.

They didn't respond, but she could see them.

Shawna tried to move around the railing towards the staircase.

She rounded the corner and then stopped as she was standing face to face with the same figure from inside the bedroom.

Shawna paused.

She could feel the hot breath of the figure in front of her, smell the decaying and rotting aroma that escaped its mouth. The figure was taller than Shawna, by nearly a foot. The body was thick and rounded, the back hunched over with long, thin arms, like branches. The face was entirely too small for the rest of the body; it had no nose, the smile had no lips, but the teeth were overwhelming. Rows and rows of yellow and crooked teeth lined the mouth. The eyes were small but perfectly round dots.

The thin twig-like arms reached out and grabbed her face, too quickly for Shawna to respond. The fingers attached to the thin arm were sharp and black with grime. One hand grabbed her by the back of her head, the other wrapped around the front of her mouth.

Shawna reacted with fists, smacking against the thin arms wrapped around her face, punching and scratching, doing whatever she could to release its grip.

The sharp fingers of the hand entered the front of her mouth, prying it open. Shawna tried to bite down, squishing the fingers in between her teeth, but the hand was too far inside her mouth before she could react. And in the blink of an eye, the hand ripped down.

Shawna didn't know what had happened, not right away.

The figure gently released the back of her head and then walked around her, up towards the bedroom. She heard the door handle jiggle before hearing it open and then close again.

She felt a warm pooling on the front of her shirt; Shawna looked down to see a red stain spreading down the front of her shirt and chest.

Shawna tried to talk but the words didn't come out. Only a gurgling sound and pain.

She reached up to her mouth, and her fingers touched the roof of the orifice.

Her eyes grew large as realization of what had happened washed over her.

On the ground in front of her, beside her feet, was the bottom of her jaw.

CHAPTER SEVEN

THIS ALL ENDS HORRIBLY | 56

Loki waited for the torture to end.

It didn't come quickly.

Arial enjoyed every moment of it.

Everytime Loki squirmed, he could feel Arial pick up the pace, or lick that much harder. Squeezing his thigh until it too, went numb.

At some point Loki lost consciousness, it was just too much for him to take.

He woke up slowly, lifting his head from the table. He inspected the room. His arms and legs were no longer strapped down. Loki tried to bend his damaged leg, but there was nothing but shocked nerves and pain as he tried. His leg was covered in blood and pus. His calf was ripped open, and shreds of skin and muscles spread out as though a grenade went off inside the limb. The thigh was scratched and cut open too. Blood still spilled out of the many puncture marks in his skin. He used his arms to brace the bottom of his leg, and slide it off the edge of the table. Loki sat there at the edge and continued to inspect the room. There she was, in the dark corner.

"We had fun," Arial said. "Didn't we?"

Loki braced himself for her to dive at him, but she didn't. He sat there for a while and thought about the question. It didn't sound like the same playfully mean voice that she had used during the entire encounter. No, it sounded different. Sorry. Remorseful. Sad. It reminded him of the few times back in another life, when Arial had upset him and apologized. Her voice was soft and small. It always broke his heart, made him want to stop fighting and wrap his arms around her, and squeeze her tight. Loki didn't have the urge to reach out and hug her at this moment, but part of him wished he could just hold her one more time.

"We used to," Loki eventually said.

Arial took a step forward, her face no longer sinister and bloody. The oozing scar on her forehead was now gone. Her makeup was as it were the last time he saw her alive, now only black streaks of mascara marred her cheeks. "That's what I'm talking about."

Loki felt his heart skip a beat.

"Remember our trip to the city? You booked us a room in a hostel?" She let a small smile climb across her face.

Loki felt a tear stream down his own, "You thought I got us a room in a brothel?"

She nodded her head up and down and smiled, a hand wiping tears from her face. "I told everyone for weeks that we had stayed at a brothel. Everyone was really confused."

"I didn't know what a hostel was, I just saw it was only seventeen bucks and thought it was a great deal!" Loki said.

Arial reached her hands out towards him. "I'm sorry we never got the opportunity to travel like we wanted to."

Loki hesitated for a moment before carefully slipping from the table and inching closer towards her. Carefully he reached his hands out for her and grabbed her open hands. "You don't have to be sorry for any of it."

The tears came more suddenly now as Arial choked on her words, "I–I really wanted to have a li–life with you. I wanted to give you everything."

Loki pulled her closer and finally wrapped his arms around her, as she pressed her face into his chest. He pulled her close and squeezed. The tears flooded from his face without hesitation. He tried to soak it all in. Loki never got the chance to say goodbye. This was all he ever wanted.

"I really loved you," Arial said. Loki could feel the words bounce off his chest.

"I know," he said.

"Thank you for showing me love while you could," she said. "I–I've never for–forgotten it."

Loki pushed back tears as he tried to reply, but the words got caught up inside his throat.

Then he felt her body shift.

He tried to hold her, but she was slipping away.

Loki released his grip and looked down at her face.

Her head ragdolled against his chest and he lifted her face to look at her.

"Arial? Arial?" He asked.

Her eyes were fogged over. Her skin slowly turned more and more pale. The wound on her forehead slowly began to open again.

"No! No! No!" Loki screamed as he tried to pull her close again, but her body was limp and hard to maneuver. Slowly, she slipped from his grip and he lowered her to the ground.

He kissed her on the cheek as the skin slowly melted down from her face and began to decompose.

Loki stood and wiped the remaining tears from his eyes. He hovered over her body for a minute and watched as she slowly decayed in front of him.

"I miss you so fucking much," Loki whispered between tears.

He turned and walked away.

Just in time to see a fist flying towards his face and connect with his eye socket.

***

Carissa had been screaming for what felt like hours.

At first she was screaming for the girls, then the guys, now she was just screaming.

Everything was black.

Dark and cramped.

She could wiggle slightly, but she felt like she was in a standing coffin.

Carissa had pounded the wall in front of her so much that her hand now hurt to the touch. She was positive it was bruised and swollen already.

She continued to scream, but even her throat began to hurt now.

She leaned her head against the wall in front of her and waited.

Carissa just wanted out.

She wanted to go back.

Go outside again, to when she was only moments away from leaving to go back home with her husband. They were going to go home and sleep before finally seeing their two small children. She hadn't held them for what felt like an eternity. She wanted to snuggle them. Kiss their faces. Smell them. Listen to them. Show them pictures. Carissa wanted to feel her baby squeeze her finger with his little baby hand wrapped around her index finger. She wanted to listen to his little baby noises as he discovered sounds. She wanted to hold her older child and play with dolls or have a tea party. Run around with her as she defied logic and stayed up way later than a toddler should be able to.

The thoughts played through her mind like a slideshow as her head pressed against the wall, until it wasn't. With no warning, the wall opened and she fell forward.

Carissa cautiously stood back up and investigated the room; even though it was mainly dark, she knew she was in one of Thomas and Shawna's spare rooms. She slowly approached the closest window, which she knew would look down over the street, pulling the blinds down enough for her to see the black minivan in the driveway. The bags were pulled out and placed beside the vehicle. Carissa dropped the blinds and looked back towards the exit of the room. Flea and Shawna sprinted into her mind. What about them? Were they okay? Had they gotten out? Were they still trapped upstairs like her? She could sneak out the window and be out, but what if that meant abandoning her friends? What about the guys? Did they get trapped inside too? She knew Loki was the first one in, but hadn't even seen him since the moment they walked inside.

Carissa took a step forward.

She needed to find her friends. Every instinct in her body told her two things: one, she could never live with herself if she left her friends behind. And two, going through the window was too easy. It had to be a trap.

Then she felt her ankle slip out from under her. Carissa crashed to the ground beside the bed. She looked down at the joint and saw a thin white hand wrapped around her foot.

Carissa screamed.

All of the screaming she did inside the little black void before was nothing compared to the scream that exited her lungs at this moment. She kicked with her free leg towards the hand, only for a second hand to fly out from under the bed, and catch that foot also. Carissa tried to pull herself free, but the hands were tight. The thing began to pull her under the bed.

Carissa rolled her body and tried to grab anything that would keep her from going under. From her knees down had disappeared beneath the bed as she squirmed and kicked to get free. Carissa managed to slip one of her feet free from her shoe, which allowed her to pull one leg out, which she braced against the frame of the bed. She extended her leg, pulling herself out from under the bed.

Soon the majority of her leg was out.

Then she saw it.

Under the bed looking back at her. A clown. A long white face, red painted cheeks, a black smile, and a round red nose. The eyes were outlined with a blue and purple design. The top of the head was bald, but both sides of the head were a mess of orange hair puffed out. Carissa wasn't afraid of clowns. She always thought the idea was hilarious. A clown is just a person. She remembered a co-worker back home had told her she was afraid of clowns, and Carissa laughed at the idea. She understood it now. She got it. The last thing she expected to see was a clown pulling her under the bed, but yet, here it was. And it was the worst possible thing she could see looking back at her.

The clown's smile crawled long across its face, keeping Carissa's full focus. Unfortunately, in doing so, she didn't pay attention to her leg braced against the bed frame. The clown ripped back on her leg, and she felt the leg that was pressed against the bed frame buckle. She watched her knee *pop* ninety degrees to the left. She heard it just as much as she felt it. Her leg was at best. dislocated at the knee, at worst broken. And with that brief moment of opportunity, the clown pulled her back under the bed. Down there the clown moved like a spider. It reached out and grabbed Carissa by her floppy leg and pulled it back towards itself. She felt the sharp pain of her leg being swung around. The popping sound echoed under the bed as the clown continued to pull her deeper under. The bed didn't seem to end, it seemed unnaturally long as she reached out for the bed frame and tried to grab anything she could. Then the clown stopped. Carissa tried to free herself, but it still hung on tightly to her ankles. Then, in the blink of an eye, the clown crawled on top of her body. She felt the heavy weight of the clown as it slid up her body and looked her in the eye. It reached out and grabbed an arm with each hand and pulled them out above her head.

"No! Please!" She screamed.

The clown tilted its head and looked at her.

"Stop! Please!" Carissa begged.

"Carissa?" a voice said from outside the cavern underneath the bed.

Carissa tried to rotate her head in that direction, but the clown was now pressing its forehead against her own.

"Carissa? Are you in here?" the voice said. It was familiar. Carissa recognized it.

"Flea! Flea! Help me!"

Carissa headbutted the clown, which caused the clown to rear its head backwards and give her the clearance to turn.

She saw Flea looking under the bed at her and the clown.

"Flea!"

Flea looked at her, then moved her focus to the clown. She smiled. "Flea! Come on!" Carissa screamed. "Come on! Please!"

Flea looked up from under the bed for a moment and then back below the bed. Carissa noticed something about her eyes. Something unusual to see in someone she had been best friends with for such a long time. Her eyes looked bright. Like a lantern glowing inside her eyeballs. Flea looked at Carissa and smirked, "You two have fun, okay?"

"No! No! Flea! Don't do this!" Carissa pleaded.

Flea stood and walked away. Carissa continued to scream as she watched her friend's feet walk around the bed, towards the door.

"Should have taken the window, Carissa," Flea said as she left the room.

"No! No! No!" Carissa screamed as she felt the clown press its weight against her body. The grip on her wrists tightened. The pain in her knee fired as the clown wiggled its way on top of her again, its full weight on top of her now.

Carissa looked up at the clown that was only inches from her face.

The clown's smile slowly spread across its face. Then slowly, its mouth opened. Two black fingers on each side of the gaping hole spread out from inside and gripped the outside of the mouth. The fingers started to pull themselves back; soon the black digits peeled back enough that all five fingers of a pitch back hand were gripping the outside of the overly stretched hand. Carissa could hear the *popping* and *cracking* sound of the mouth expanding and widening. The jaw of the clown was now at least a foot wide, its white makeup smeared and rubbed down to the same ashy gray of the flesh around the jaw. The black hands released from around the mouth of the clown and then reached out towards Carissa.

She shook her head as violently as she could, but there was no use. Her arms were spread out above her head, and the weight upon her body made it impossible. The black hands wrapped around her head until she was fully cradled by them. Then slowly, the hands started to retract, pulling her head into the open mouth of the clown.

She shook her head, but it was useless.

The last sound she heard before her head was fully inside the mouth of the clown was Flea laughing outside the door.

Then everything hurt as she felt the clown chomp down on her head.

And then her body went limp.

CHAPTER *EIGHT*

THIS ALL ENDS HORRIBLY | 64

"Oh, fuck!" Derek screamed as he watched Loki fall to the floor. Derek pulled back his fist and rushed down to his friend that he had just punched in the face.

Loki had instinctively braced his face for another assault, but both Derek and Tyler were there to pull Loki up before he had fully rolled to the ground.

Derek and Tyler each took one of Loki's arms and pulled him to his feet.

"Holy shit, dude," Tyler said. "What happened to your leg?"

Loki looked down at the injury that Derek hadn't noticed at first, "A lot." He said.

Derek could see the bloody mess, it dangled almost lifelessly before him. Tyler threw one of Loki's arms around his shoulder to brace him.

"We need to get out of here," Loki said, as Derek noticed his eye socket begin to bruise.

"I'm sorry, Loki," Derek said. "We heard some noise and went to investigate, and with everything we've seen in here, I just reacted."

Loki shook his head, "Dude, it's fine. Get us out of here and get me a really large beer, and we will be even."

"Deal," Tyler said as he readjusted Loki's arm around his shoulder in order to carry more of his weight.

"What's the plan?" Loki asked.

"We need to get Thomas's phone. We think it'll access the security camera and we can see what the hell started all of this," Derek said as they moved in the direction of the front door.

"Where's Thomas?" Loki asked.

Derek shot a look over to Tyler, who caught his gaze.

"Listen–" Derek started.

Loki shook his head, "No, don't. I can put the pieces together. Why do we have to get his phone? Why can't we just leave?"

Tyler shrugged, "Last time we *tried* to just leave… Thomas… Well, what happened, happened then."

"So leaving isn't an option?" Loki asked.

"We don't know, but we also don't want to risk it again, not until we find the phone and get some answers," Derek said. "Plus, we still don't know if the girls are here or not. They haven't answered our calls for them, but we are pretty sure that doesn't mean anything."

"I didn't hear you screaming for them," Loki said.

"Exactly. The girls might not have either," Tyler said. "So we need to get the phone, get the girls, and then go from there."

"I hate it," Loki said.

"Me too," Derek said.

"Sounds like a horrible plan," Loki said.

"Agreed," Tyler said.

"So let's get going," Loki said as he took a painful step forward with Tyler.

The men slowly walked towards the front door. Derek led the way, making sure they weren't about to fall into another trap.

There he was.

Thomas, in a pool of blood, just as they had left him.

"Loki, don't look," Derek said. He wanted to make sure that Loki didn't see the state of one of his best friends. Fucking hell, Thomas was the entire reason he had made the move to Oregon. Packed up whatever bit he had left of his life and started again with dreams of creating comic books with Thomas.

Derek turned and watched Loki turn his head.

He then kneeled down in front of his fallen friend and dug around until he came across a phone in his pocket.

"Got it!" Derek said.

"Fuck yes!" Tyler exclaimed. "I thought he left it in the car or something so that's lucky."

"Yeah," Derek agreed as he pushed the phone into his own pocket. "Now," he looked up towards the staircase, "let's go find the girls."

***

Flea could feel the haze lifting.

Like a fog that slowly rose from around her. Gradually, she came back to the present. She stood in the kids bathroom, looking face to face with the mirror.

She could remember certain things after being sucked into the light, but not all of it. She remembered that something was in the room with her. Flea could recall walking around the upstairs, going room to room for some reason. She spent a lot of time in one of the rooms, although it wasn't clear to her why, or what she did in there.

Flea reached out and laid each hand on the counter.

She didn't have control over her body yet, the fog was still dissipating, but wasn't completely gone. She tried to move her hands, but couldn't. Flea looked up at the mirror and found herself looking back.

The reflection tilted its head and smiled back at her.

"Wakey, wakey," her reflection said back at her.

Flea struggled to move her hands, but it was useless. She tried not to focus on the reflection.

"Don't fight. I'm not done with you. Not yet."

Flea felt one of her hands move across the bathroom counter. The middle and index finger up, as if they were walking. Playing with her. The hand reached the edge of the counter and opened up a small drawer. It pulled out a thick pair of nail clippers and brought them back towards her.

"I can feel you pushing away. I can tell our time left together is short," the reflection said. "I've got to make the most of it."

Flea looked down and watched as the clippers opened up and aimed from one hand, towards the fingers of her other hand.

"This is gonna be pretty awful," the reflection said. "I am going to make sure of it."

Flea tried to look away, but she had no control. The clippers tightly squeezed against the long nail of her thumb, right at the base, closest to the end. A million things ran through her head as the clippers squeezed, but didn't *clip* off her nail. Instead, they gripped into her nail hard enough to pinch the nail with as much force as possible, yet didn't clip through. Then the hand with the clippers and her other hand began to slowly separate from each other; pulling the nail out from underneath her skin. She could feel it rip away from her thumb savagely.

The nerve endings were now exposed to the air, blood shooting from the exposed tips of her thumb. Flea wanted to scream. She wanted to say every curse word she had ever heard, but she couldn't. She watched as the clipper dropped the entire bloody nail on the counter. Then the clipper moved towards her index finger. Again, it reached as far up as it could and squeezed against the nail until it had a good grip, then it pulled. Flea again felt the nail rip from her skin and pop out from her flesh. Blood pooled beneath her hand onto the counter, as the clipper dropped the nail and moved on to the next finger.

Then it was over.

Flea felt the fog completely lift.

She fell to the floor of the bathroom and cried. She grabbed her hand and brought it to her chest. With her free hand she grabbed the towel off the rack beside her and wrapped it tightly around her hand.

Flea could hear the reflection in the mirror laughing at her.

She gritted her teeth as she wrapped her hand tightly.

"Jokes on you," Flea said. "I hated those. Now I just have an excuse to get them redone when I get out of here."

She stood up and looked at her reflection in the mirror. The reflection continued to laugh at her.

Flea tilted her head and looked at the reflection for a moment before raising her wrapped hand. "You left me my favorite finger, anyways." Flea lifted her middle finger at her reflection and smiled. "Fuck you, bitch."

She turned and walked out of the bathroom.

***

Tyler slowly made his way up the staircase with Loki leaning against him.

Tyler wasn't a small man, he was more than able to help Loki as much as he needed. They talked about leaving Loki behind with Thomas, but that seemed like a bad idea. Sure, walking wasn't going to be easy for him, and he could slow the rest of the group down. However, they didn't know if that would leave Loki too vulnerable to whatever else was thrown at him. Instead, they decided to stick together.

Slowly, they climbed the staircase.

Derek led the way, only a couple steps ahead of them. As he approached the landing, he paused and looked down at the ground. "Fuck," he said softly before he looked down at Tyler and Loki. "It's Shawna."

"Goddamnit," Loki muttered to himself.

Derek reached down and Tyler could see he was checking her pulse. He then turned back and shook his head, *no*.

"Keep going," Tyler said. "We need to find the others."

Derek paused for a moment before carrying on to his left.

Tyler slowly moved Loki forward, up to the landing.

Once there, he did his best not to look down at his friend below him.

He felt his foot kick something and looked down in spite of himself.

It took a moment for it to register, but eventually he realized it was Shawna's jaw.

Tyler closed his eyes tight and continued forward behind Derek.

He had stopped at the master bedroom, his hands clasping the doorknob.

"What are you waiting for?" Tyler asked.

Derek took a moment to answer, before looking back at Tyler, "I'm scared of what's behind this door."

"Me too," Tyler admitted. "I'm afraid of finding–" he trailed off.

"Yeah, me too," Derek said.

"The girls?" Loki asked. "Right? You guys are afraid of finding the girls like *that*?" He said with a finger pointing towards Shawna.

Tyler and Derek didn't respond.

"I'll open the door," Loki said.

"No, I can do it," Derek said.

"I know you can," Loki said. "But you don't have to. Let me look first and tell you whether or not it's something we need to worry about. Just let me, please."

Derek looked from Loki over to Tyler.

Tyler didn't know the right answer.

He was terrified to open the door. To see his wife in a pool of blood, with something awful having happened to her. He couldn't do it, and wondered if Derek doing it was a good idea or not. Eventually he nodded his head, telling Derek he should step aside.

Derek moved out of the way with a lowered head. Defeated. Scared.

Loki reached out to the doorknob and grabbed it, about to twist. "You guys ready?"

Tyler nodded his head.

"Oh my god!" He heard from behind him.

Tyler flung his body around in time to see his wife sprinting towards him. Flea jumped through the air and wrapped her body around Tyler. Tyler began pouring kisses all over her face as he held her tight.

"Oh my god, Tyler! Oh, my god!" Tears began streaming down her face as her body began to quiver.

CHAPTER NINE

THIS ALL ENDS HORRIBLY | 72

Derek watched as his best friend held his wife.

He was overcome with emotion, and a single tear slipped from his eye.

Derek reached out and wrapped his arms around them both.

He felt Flea's hand, wrapped in a bloody towel, reach out and hold onto him.

"I'm so happy you're okay," Derek said as Tyler and Flea finished their embrace. "We need to get moving though. Where's Carissa?"

Flea's face dropped.

She shook her head, "I–I don't know."

Tyler reached out and grabbed him by the shoulder, "Doesn't mean she's gone. We are going to find her."

"Yeah, that doesn't mean anything. We can still get her," Loki agreed.

Derek felt dread crawl back into his brain again.

The idea of opening a door to his wife lifeless.

He tried to shake it off.

"Listen, I'm going to give you the phone," Derek said. "You guys try to get on the security cameras. I'm going to look in each room for my wife."

Derek pulled out the phone he retrieved from Thomas's pocket and gave it to Loki.

"I should only be a minute," Derek said as he turned down the hall towards the bedrooms and laundry room.

He moved to the furthest room and carefully opened the door.

Derek hadn't been inside the room often; it was the spare room. Carissa and he had crashed on the spare bed a couple times, but for the most part, they slept on the couch downstairs after a long night out with everyone. He wanted to do a quick sweep, but nothing *too* fast. Yet he didn't want to be away from the group terribly long. He still had another four bedrooms, as well as the laundry room and bathroom to check.

Though every part of his being screamed to not separate at all–Derek had seen enough scary movies to know that this was never a good idea. He moved towards the window and pulled down a blind to peek outside. Life looked normal out there. The van was still waiting for them in the driveway, the luggage was still where they left it.

Derek turned to leave the room.

Everything seemed normal in there.

No sign of his wife.

Derek took a step forward and felt his foot *squish* in the carpet. He lifted his foot and saw a pool of blood coming from under the bed.

Without a moment to think, Derek threw himself to the ground and lifted away the bedsheet so he could look underneath.

There she was.

Her head in the mouth of a clown as it chewed.

Derek didn't hesitate. He lifted the mattress from its frame and hurled it across the room.

He lunged towards the clown and threw his shoulder into it. He felt the electric pain in his shoulder. Derek had broken something, his shoulder instantly went numb and his arm tingled, but it didn't stop him. He drove his foot into the ground and kept going.

"Oh, my god," Derek screamed.

The clown flinched.

"Oh. My. GOD!" Derek screamed again as he dug his feet into the ground and continued to push his shoulder against the clown with its mouth wrapped around his wife. "Oh my fucking god!" he screamed as the last burst of energy pulsed through him. He felt the *click* of the clown's jaw and that gave him enough drive to keep pushing. As Derek drove his foot into the ground and lowered his shoulder again, he felt the clown buckle under his pressure.

"Der–" Derek heard beneath him.

He looked down and saw his wife, her face mangled and deformed. Mauled as if a pack of ravenous dogs had closed in on her and chewed her face for fun.

"I'm here, baby. I'm here," Derek cupped her head. He used his leg to push the clown further into the darkness.

Derek grabbed his wife and pulled her out from under the bed.

Soon enough, he could see the extent of the damage. Her face was chewed beyond comprehension. The entirety of her head was swollen and bruised. Blood streamed down her sad face, and Derek didn't know how to react. He froze.

"I didn't let it," Carissa tried to say," I didn't let it–"

"Don't," Derek interrupted. "Don't."

Carissa pushed him aside, even though she was weak and drained of energy, "I didn't let it eat me."

Derek smirked, "No, you didn't. You didn't let it eat you, honey."

Carissa smiled as her chest rose and fell. Her breathing became shallow as she closed her swollen eyes.

Derek knew that their time was running out.

She wasn't going to last much longer.

As Derek cradled his wife, he heard movement from across the room. He was so distracted with Carissa that he had completely forgotten about the monster that was trying to swallow her like an anaconda in the rainforest.

He turned in time to see the clown get to its feet.

The smile on its painted face was stretched wide, the paint was smeared and cracked. Teeth that looked like needles, thousands of needles, lined the gums of the twisted clown.

Derek rose to his feet and braced himself for the attack.

The clown crouched to the ground, its hands out on the floor and its face looking towards Derek and Carissa. It looked like a spider about to fling itself out towards its meal.

Derek looked for anything around him that he could use to protect himself. Nothing screamed out to him as a viable weapon.

Derek watched as the clown crawled around to the center of the room, leaving Derek and Carissa's unconscious body cornered.

"Fuck this," Derek said.

He closed his fists and rolled his shoulders. A sharp pain shot through his body, reminding him of the damage he received only minutes ago.

Still, he lowered his frame and sprinted towards the creature.

CHAPTER TEN

THIS ALL ENDS HORRIBLY | 76

"It wasn't like this," Flea said as they entered Thomas and Shawna's master bedroom. The room was no longer empty, but looked old and lived in. The walls were splattered with red, which Flea assumed was blood. The light in the center of the room was no longer a beacon that made Flea feel like she was a magnet being pulled towards it. It was a simple light fixture attached to a ceiling fan. The bed was tossed, as if someone had just woken up and left it as is. However, knowing Shawna, it was more likely that this was the normal state of the bed on a daily basis.

"I know all about that," Tyler said as he picked up a small figurine from Shawna's desk, inspected it and placed it back down. "Things can change in the blink of an eye. Let's just give it a look and move on."

"The phone," Loki reminded the group.

"Fucking hell," Tyler said as he reached back inside his pocket and pulled out the phone that Derek had recovered on Thomas's body. "I forgot."

Tyler pressed the button on the side of the phone, and the phone illuminated back to life. "Wait," Tyler said.

Flea finished looking over the bathroom; everything seemed more than normal, except the blood slowly sliding down the wall like fresh paint. Flea was tempted to touch it, see if it was actually *was* blood, but she didn't. What would be the point? It wouldn't change anything, and would probably appear as blood whether it was or not. She turned back towards her husband, "What?"

Tyler turned the phone towards her. She could see what he was confused about. Instead of a background of the San Francisco 49ers, it was a picture of Derek and Carissa on a locked screen.

"That's Derek's phone," Flea said.

"I know," Tyler confirmed.

"Why did he give you his phone?" Loki asked.

"I don't know," Tyler said. "I don't think it was on purpose."

"He pulled that phone off Thomas's body, didn't he?" Loki asked.

Tyler thought about it for a moment, "Yeah, I think so. I think Thomas had borrowed Derek's phone earlier. He must have never given it back."

"Well, shit," Loki said. "Guess this was a dud."

"What was the point of getting on Thomas's phone again?" Flea asked.

Tyler knew Derek's pin to access the phone, 1006... his wife's birthday. He opened the phone before trying to dial out. After a moment he put the phone back in his pocket, "Useless."

"What was the point of getting Thomas's phone?" Flea repeated, her voice holding a hint of annoyance at having to ask again.

Tyler looked back to his wife, "Sorry. We wanted to access his security system and see what happened while we were gone."

"Well, what about Shawna's phone?" Flea asked.

Tyler didn't change his expression.

His face was flat and expressionless.

"Fuck," Tyler finally said. "I feel fucking stupid that I didn't think of that."

"Idiot," Loki said as he left the room and went back towards Shawna's body.

"You didn't think of it either," Tyler said loud enough that Loki could hear him, but not loud enough that it was yelled.

Tyler walked around the room, looking it over. "You know, we haven't spent much time up here."

Flea chuckled, "Why would we? It's *their* room."

"I know," Tyler said. "But we have known them for years, and we spend every Tuesday together. Most weekends together. We know them better than anyone else. I just think it's funny that we weren't allowed to see their room."

Flea rolled her eyes, "It wasn't that we weren't *allowed to*... just we didn't. Why would we?"

Tyler shrugged, "I don't know. I was just trying to think of something to say. Tried to get our mind off of whatever the hell this is that's going on. Only if for a moment, I wanted to escape."

Flea smiled, "I get it." She walked around the bed and towards her husband. She grabbed each of his hands in her own, "Thank you. I needed that."

She kissed him.

"Got it," Loki said as he entered the room and tossed it towards Tyler.

Tyler caught it, "Any sign of Derek or Carissa while you were out there?"

Loki shook his head, "Not that I noticed. But I also wasn't looking. Was kinda focusing on my hand digging around the pockets of one of my closest friends' dead body."

Tyler nodded his head and brought the phone up to his face, "Passcode?" He asked in Flea's direction.

"Their anniversary," Flea said. "I know that much."

"Cool," Tyler looked up from the phone. "What's that?"

Flea thought about it for a moment. She could remember the event. It was summer. Hot. A small wedding, only close friends and family at a park. However, the actual date escaped her. She shrugged.

"Seriously?" Loki said as he limped over to the phone and typed in the pin. "0713."

"Oh, that sounds about right," Flea acknowledged.

Loki turned the phone, showing that it was opened. "It was."

Loki scrolled the phone to the apps section, continuing until he saw something that looked like it was a security app. "Any idea what we are looking for here?"

"Not really," Tyler admitted. "We just need to find whatever app the cameras are attached to."

"Do you know the brand?" Loki asked.

Tyler shook his head, "Just scroll. Can't be too many. Look for something that says *smart* or *security*."

Loki continued scrolling.

Flea turned and looked around the room.

Shawna's desk.

Flea walked over and moved the mouse; the desktop came to life.

On the front of the desktop was a little icon.

A blue box with the words: Roz Security.

She double clicked it.

A window opened. She had found it.

"Guys," Flea said. She felt the men turn towards her and approach her.

"Great job, babe," Tyler said.

"Yeah," Loki agreed. "Making us really look like amateurs here."

Flea clicked on the tab that said LOG. A little red dot beside the word told Flea that there was unchecked footage.

"Let's see what we are up against," she said.

***

Derek had taken some hits.

He could feel his face swelling. Bruising. Bleeding.

It had been easier when the clown was wedged under the bed. Now that it was out in the open, that wasn't the case. It was powerful. Strong. Towering.

The clown paced around Derek in a semi-circle. Toying with him.

Derek lunged his body out towards the creature, but was met with it gripping him, tossing him over its shoulder, and his body slamming against the wall of the bedroom.

Derek slid to the ground, drywall and chipped paint falling with him. He stood and brushed himself off. He wasn't about to quit now.

He assessed the room around him. It was tossed. The nightstand ripped open. Paper and books lay ripped open and scattered. The lamp that used to sit on top of the nightstand was snapped and broken. A TV on a tall dresser had fallen and folded in half on the ground. The bed frame was made of wood. Sturdy. The old type of frame that Derek could imagine his step-dad saying "they don't make em like this anymore" about, if he was around.

Derek lifted his foot and smashed it down on the frame. He continued to slam down until it snapped. Derek quickly picked it up before the clown could close in.

He turned around to an empty room. The mess that was there only seconds ago was now gone. Even the bed frame he had snapped was miraculously gone. The piece in his hand was the only proof that it ever existed.

The closet door slowly opened.

EEEEEEEICH it screeched slowly.

Derek prepared himself, holding the snapped piece of wood out like a lance.

He wasn't prepared for the speed of what sprang from the closet. A pitch black hand stretched out from the bottom of the closet and gripped Derek's ankle. It snapped back towards the closet just as fast, knocking Derek to the floor.

He looked down and saw the dark black hand pulling him towards the clown.

The clown sat on the floor, cross legged, with its mouth wide open. The arm was coming out of its mouth! Stretched out like the tongue of a frog, it pulled Derek's leg towards it.

Derek realized he no longer had the piece of wood in his hands and reached back to grab it, but failed. It was too far. Derek sat up and tried to free his ankle, but the jet black hand wrapped around it didn't budge, it gripped harder. Derek flung his fists at the hand; connecting with it was like punching a rock. It was impossible to damage. It hurt his fist immediately, but Derek couldn't stop. He continued to throw fist after fist, hoping that it would free him from the clown's weird mouth-hand.

"Fucking-fuck! Let! Me! Go!" Derek screamed as he punched over and over again.

Derek's foot was now only inches away from entering the clown's open mouth. He had walked in on it swallowing his wife, he knew that it was more than capable of unhinging its jaw and swallowing him.

"There is no way this is how I go out!" Derek said to himself. "Eaten by a fucking clown? Are you kidding me?" He kicked down at the clown's face with his free foot.

He could feel his foot bounce off the clown's nose and Derek heard a *popping* noise as it connected. Derek continued to kick again and again. With each blow there was another *pop* or *crack*.

Then the clown reached out with one of its hands and grabbed his leg, mid air. Derek reached out for the frame of the door, trying to use it to keep himself from being pulled into the clown's mouth.

However, the clown was stronger. Much stronger. He couldn't grip hard enough that it did any good. He continued being pulled towards the open mouth of the clown.

Derek could feel it as his foot entered the mouth, the hand around his ankle pulling it down. The sharp needle-like teeth getting caught on his pants and ripping them before finding his bare skin and shredding his legs.

Then, with almost no warning, the clown's face flung backwards. Something had struck it.

Derek turned around and saw his wife with the broken piece of bed frame. She swung it out towards the clown and smashed it into its face. The snapped piece of wood pierced into the skull with a deafening wet *thunk*! She pulled the wood back, blood spraying from the hole in its face, and then jammed it back. Again and again, until Derek felt the body of the clown fall limp and release his ankle from its grasp.

CHAPTER ELEVEN

THIS ALL ENDS HORRIBLY | 84

Tyler watched over Flea's shoulder.

He watched as she cautiously clicked on the unchecked messages.

Several screenshots of the last couple of days popped up on the screen. Flea turned around to the boys and then back to the monitor. She moved the mouse over, and clicked the most recent.

It was a video that was activated when the men were last downstairs. They could be seen walking around through the window in the front door. The men continued to walk in circles for a moment before going upstairs.

"That was only a couple minutes ago," Tyler said. "That's when Derek grabbed the phone off Thomas."

"So he has a couple cameras, anything on the inside?" Loki asked.

Flea clicked a couple tabs and shook her head, "No, he has a doorbell cam, a camera that faces towards the door, and another that looks over his driveway."

"Well, shit," Tyler said.

"At least there's something," Flea said as she clicked the next video.

The men again stood around, walking by the window.

"When was that?" Flea asked.

Tyler and Loki both leaned in.

"Hard to tell," Loki said.

"Yeah, I don't know, to be honest," Tyler said. He tried to see what was happening. He didn't see Loki, so he knew it was before they had found him.

Then Thomas walked into view and Tyler knew exactly when this was.

"Skip this video," Tyler said quickly.

"What?" Flea asked.

"Now!" Tyler said as fast as he could, grabbing the mouse from Flea and clicking away.

"Whoa," Loki said. "Calm down, champ. What was that about?"

Tyler took a couple deep breaths and tried to calm down as Loki suggested, "Sorry. Sorry. That was–"

"That was when Thomas died... wasn't it?" Flea finished it for him.

Tyler felt the tear roll down his cheek, he brushed it away with the top of his hand. "Yeah, I couldn't watch it again."

Flea reached out for his hand and grabbed it tightly.

"Come on," Tyler said as he released his wife's hand. "Keep going."

Flea grabbed the mouse back and skipped to the next video.

Tyler, Thomas, and Derek walked into the house.

"Fuck," Loki said. "Bet you wish you guys could take that one back?"

"Hardy-har-har," Tyler mock laughed.

"And there's the girls and Loki," Flea said as she skipped to the next video.

"How many videos are left?" Loki asked.

Flea clicked back to the inbox, "Several."

She clicked the next one, the arrival of the van from the trip.

"Look at those fools," Loki said. "About to walk into hell, and they were worried about pissing their pants before they even entered."

Flea clicked out and onto the next one. Movement from the window in the front door. Through the window they could see a painting that was centered on the back wall throw itself out of frame.

"So this was happening before we showed up," Tyler said as he leaned forward.

The next video.

A black shadow walks slowly across the frame, stops in the center of the window and then turns around and slowly walks back out.

The next video.

A head slowly pops around the corner of the frame, a child's head, it giggles and then ducks back out of frame.

"What's going on?" Flea asked.

"It's waiting," Tyler said.

"For what?" Loki asked.

"For someone to come home," Tyler stated.

In the next video, a postman walked up and placed a couple of boxes at the door.

"Wait," Tyler said. "Was there already a package at the door when he showed up?"

Flea restarted the video, it was a quick video, the postman was only in frame for a moment, and he was already in the middle of placing the box when it started. However, it looked like he was placing the packages on top of another box. A box that was already at the door.

"Next video," Tyler said.

As Flea clicked the next video, again, there was movement inside the house from the window. A body fell from the ceiling, bare feet up to the knees in frame. The body wiggled as it fought, before it finally flinched one last time, and stopped.

"Was that–" Loki began to ask.

"Yes it was," Flea answered.

"So someone just hung themselves?" Loki continued.

They ignored him and watched as the lifeless feet rotated slowly in the room, before the body was pulled out of the frame in a blink of an eye.

They all took a deep breath.

Video after video of something different in front of the front window.

Every video was unexpected and different from the last. In one video, a man walked up to the window and began to eat his own fingers. One at a time, he took a bite of each digit and painfully ripped it from his hand. Blood splashed onto his face as he chewed the finger and then moved on to the next one. In another video, a woman walked up and held a baby to the glass, Flea clicked that video away before they could see what happened next. In yet another video, a man stood still at the window for what felt like hours, before he reached into his pocket and pulled out a pencil, pulling it up towards his eyes faster than Flea could click away.

Finally, there was something different. Three days earlier, the group watched as someone came and placed the package at their doorstep.

"That's not a postal worker," Flea said. "Plus, it's in the middle of the night."

"Do you remember that package?" Loki asked.

Flea nodded, "Yeah, I think so."

"Then let's go see what's inside it," Tyler said.

***

Derek slowly pulled himself up from the ground and limped over to his wife. Carissa dropped the snapped bed frame and put a hand out for Derek to lift her.

He reached down and pulled her up, embracing her with both arms, squeezing as tight as he could.

Derek was terrified about everything that happened to the group tonight. Walking into a kitchen full of rotting corpses will do that to a person. Watching one of your best friends' faces ripped off will too. However, nothing scared him more than when he pulled the sheets back from the bed and saw his wife's head stuck inside the mouth of a clown. Derek was scared she was gone. He was too late. He had failed her.

Turns out, not only did she pull through, but *she* ended up being the one that saved *him*.

Derek slowly kissed her on the forehead. His lips pressed against the swollen, bruised, and bloodied face. Her eyes were barely open, as they were extremely swollen and bruised. She looked like she had a horrible allergic reaction while fighting away a porcupine.

He released her and wrapped her arm around his shoulder, then together they walked out of the room.

Derek opened the door and they limped out into the hallway.

"Derek?" A voice said softly in his ear.

He turned and saw nothing.

"You hear that?" Derek asked.

"No," Carissa responded.

"Derek?" the voice whispered again.

"Are you sur–" Derek turned to his wife to ask again, before he saw it.

Directly behind her shoulder was a pale white face. Long, stringy black hair parted in the middle and ran down both sides. Wide eyes that were entirely too large for a human face and looked like bad AI art. Finally, he saw the mouth that stretched further into a smile than any person should reasonably be able to smile.

As he stared at the face above his wife's shoulder, the smile stretched further and further.

"I have you," it whispered.

Derek couldn't look away. He tried, but his body wouldn't let him budge. He felt his eyes water as he realized he wasn't blinking. Derek was focused solely on the woman's face.

"You guys!" Derek heard from down the hallway behind him.

He felt Carissa let go of him and run over to what he *assumed* was the rest of the group.

"He did it! He found you!" A squeaky female voice said, which Derek assumed was Flea. However everything seemed compressed. As if they were down a long tunnel or in the background of a park.

He continued to hear them talk and cry. Derek wanted to turn and join them, but he was no longer in control and he knew it.

Now that Carissa had moved, he could see the entirety of the body that the head was attached to. It was gangly, thin, and pale. The body looked like it was a shrink wrapped skeleton. A black night dress draped over the body. The toenails were long and yellow, however the fingernails looked like they had been chewed to a sliver. The woman's fingertips were raw and bleeding.

"Derek, come on," Tyler said.

Derek tried as hard as he could and felt the entity lifting him, like a weight attached to a chain around his neck. With all of his might he fought and twisted his head towards the group.

There, at the end of the hallway were all of his friends; all with stretched smiles, their eyes inhumanly large.

He felt a tap on his shoulder.

"What is he doing?" Derek heard Flea ask. Although he couldn't see her, he knew she was still standing at the end of the hallway.

Derek felt the weight attached to the chain around his neck pull his head back away from his friends; he tried to stop it, but he couldn't

Derek blinked away a single tear as he felt the rush of control leave his body.

Like a tidal wave, he felt the control roll away.

The woman's head popped out again and whispered into his ear, "There." Derek saw a long, bone-thin finger point over his shoulder and towards the wall.

Derek moved as though propelled; he couldn't fight it. His legs move without his permission.

"Oh no," he heard Flea say quietly.

Derek walked over to the wall and lifted both arms to eye level, grabbing picture frame of Shawna and Thomas on their wedding day. He dropped it to the ground, and the glass shattered at his feet.

Derek tried to understand what was about to happen.

He heard his feet smash the glass in the picture frame beneath his feet. Wa he going to pick up the glass? Was he going to use it on himself? His friends Derek tried once again to fight back, but nothing happened.

"What? What is he doing, Flea?" Carissa asked, Derek could clearly hear th panic in her voice escalate.

"He isn't doing this," Flea said flatly.

Derek raised his hands against the wall at shoulder width.

Then Derek saw it.

A single nail in the wall. The same nail that only moments ago, held the picture from a beautiful day.

Before Derek could fully question whether Thomas was the kind of guy that would hammer a nail into a stud for a picture frame, he had thrown his head backwards and forwards at full speed.

Thunk.

Derek felt it.

He felt the head of the nail bounce violently against his skull.

It hurt. It hurt so fucking bad.

Again Derek threw his head back and forward.

Over and over.

By the time his friends had reached him to hold him back, Derek could fee the head of the nail force itself through his forehead and shatter bone. Warm blood oozed down his face and obscured his vision.

"Oh my god, oh my god, oh my god," he heard Carissa repeat over and over.

He felt the strong grip of Loki and Tyler on his shoulders as he was pulled away from the wall. His body didn't seem to fight.

He collapsed to the ground, into his wife's lap.

Derek felt a hand rub against his face, pushing some of the blood from his sight.

There they were no longer hidden from him.

Carissa grabbed one of his hands and kissed it. "Derek, we are going to get out of here. We have to keep fighting. We are going to do this, I promise."

Derek tried to talk, and to his surprise his mouth moved. He tried a couple more times before he was able to say, "I know. I-I love you."

Carissa smiled through her bruised and swollen face.

Then the smile quickly fell flat. Her eyes grew large in fear.

Derek looked down and saw his other hand beneath her jaw. Blood covered his hands as it rushed out of Carissa's body.

He pulled his hand back towards himself and saw a large blade of glass in his grip.

"N-n-no," Derek said softly.

Then he felt pressure on his neck.

Like he was being attacked by bees. Over and over.

He felt the warmth of blood leaving his body.

Derek looked down and saw the glass shard in his hand still, as it repeatedly jabbed into his neck. Blood sprayed from his neck and also filled his lungs.

Everything turned to black as his brain wrapped around everything that had just happened. He had killed his wife and then himself. They weren't walking away.

As the final curtain of black was pulled over his vision, he saw the thin gangly hand wrapped around his wrist, puppeting the shard of glass towards his face.

CHAPTER TWELVE

THIS ALL ENDS HORRIBLY | 92

No one moved.

Tyler and Flea stood there frozen, for what Loki felt was an eternity.

It had all happened so fast.

Loki had watched Carissa embrace her husband. One second she was kissing his hand, and the next she had fallen forward in a pool of her own blood. As Loki had tried to understand what had already happened, he watched as Derek repeatedly jabbed a shard of glass into his own throat.

Now, the group stood and waited.

Were they waiting for their turn?

Was it easier to just give in, and let it happen?

All the pain. All the torture that had been thrown at them; was it really better to survive? How would they even explain what had happened to them? Loki couldn't imagine a situation where he was able to explain to the police that he wasn't responsible for the gruesome murders inside the house. *"No, sir, you don't understand… I had to take a shit. I didn't even want to go inside that house."*

Loki shook his head.

"We need to go," he finally said.

Tyler looked over to him and nodded, "He's right, babe. We gotta move."

Together, they helped Flea down the stairs. She wasn't crying. She wasn't doing much of anything. Her body was simply in shock from what she'd witnessed. One step at a time, they moved down the staircase.

"You said the boxes were down here?" Loki asked Flea.

Flea didn't answer.

"Yeah," Tyler answered after enough time had passed for Flea to respond. "She said they collected them when they came inside."

Loki tried not to look around. He knew that whatever was waiting for them downstairs was not any better than what they had just walked away from. He focused on the steps in front of them and nothing else. Before he knew it, they were on the ground floor; together they moved Flea around to the front room.

"There it is," Loki said as he pointed towards the stack of boxes on the coffee table. A collection of Amazon and USPS boxes were stacked with a smaller box on top. The smaller box on top was a standard cardboard box that had been duct taped shut. Unlabelled. No postage.

Loki reached over and grabbed it as Tyler led his wife to the couch.

Loki held the box in one hand, "I guess… I fucking open it, right?"

"No, I want you to actually wrap it in some wrapping paper, put a little bow on it, and then let's wait for Christmas, and put it under the fucking tree," Tyler said with all the anger from the night boiling over. "Yes, I want you to fucking open it!" Tyler dug in his pocket and pulled out a pocket knife, tossing it in the air to Loki.

Loki fumbled while catching it, but did. He opened the blade and lined it up with the tape. "I feel like that was unnecessary," Loki said. "Kinda rude."

Tyler chuckled. "What?"

Loki pulled the knife down the tape and slit the box open, "I don't think you need to be cursing at me, ya know? You're really just letting the house win."

"Oh, yeah? How so?" Tyler said with a hint of playfulness in his voice.

"I mean, the house has been a dick to us all night. I think us being rude to each other is exactly what the house wants," Loki smiled. "Fucking don't want that."

"I'm sorry. What do you want me to say next time?" Tyler asked.

Loki sat down beside them on the couch.

"Tartar-sauce," Flea said softly.

"Tartar-sauce?" Tyler laughed as he wrapped his arms around his wife.

"I make the kids say it in my class, it's a good filler word for *fuck*," she said.

Loki watched as Flea seemed to snap back to the moment. Given the situation, it was surprisingly fast; however, there really wasn't much time to sit and think about what was happening around them, Loki figured.

"Okay, tartar-sauce it is," Loki said. "Now let's see what we have in here."

Tyler watched as Loki opened the box.

He didn't know what he expected to happen. A bright light? Spirits to jump out? Hell, he wouldn't have be surprised if a fucking jack-in-the-box popped out. However, what actually happened was impressively lame.

Nothing.

Loki reached inside the box, "We got—" he said as he pulled out two items.

Tyler raised a brow. "A tape recorder and a square?"

Loki tossed the square over to Tyler and kept the tape recorder to himself, "Yeah, I don't know. This tape recorder is old. I mean *old-old*. Old cassette tape and everything."

Tyler caught the square and investigated it immediately.

It wasn't actually a square; not really. If anything, it was closer to a handmade frame. Four thin pieces of blackened wood attached together at two forty-five degree angles to make a perfect ninety. As Tyler investigated it further, he saw there were words etched along the side of the frame. Not etched, carved.

Click.

Tyler turned his attention to Loki as he pressed play on the tape recorder.

A voice began to sound from the machine; at first it was warped and hard to hear. It sounded to Tyler like the voice was melted and oozing through the small speakers on the ancient device. Eventually, the voice came back and it sounded normal. An older man. His voice made Tyler feel safe and secure. For a moment, even just a slight one, he forgot that he had watched his best friends in the world die in front of him. The voice said, "crazy might be saying it loosely. I know how this all sounds, trust me, I do. You are in danger. The second you were gifted this artifact, you and anyone around will die."

Tyler shot a look over to Loki, who was already locked in with him.

The voice continued, "The frame opens a gateway to hell on Earth, as far as we can tell. It was given to us by someone trying to save their own ass. They explained the rules. They left. And after a few deaths we realized this was real. Hell is seeping in through this hole. Look through it and you will see. What's inside that frame is nothing less than evil."

Tyler gripped his hands around the frame tightly.

"You have two choices, neither of which are pleasant. If you say the blasphemy scratched into the wood it will allow you time to move the artifact. It will pause for three hours as you find the next host. Once there, the artifact will restart, opening slowly over three days and squeezing out the evil into our world. You will be in the clear, or at least your physical form will be. Your mind will be haunted forever for what you did, and who you did it too. There is also the matter of explaining to the authorities what happened to your loved ones. The other option is to let it kill you. Once it has killed everyone within its reach it will go dormant. Waiting to be moved, then it will start the cycle again."

Tyler exhaled a long breath that he hadn't even realized he was holding.

"I don't know what else to tell you. Good luck, I guess. And god have mercy on everyone's soul who touches this goddamn curse."

Tyler heard sobbing alongside the main voice. The old man wasn't alone, someone younger was with him. Whoever it was began crying, softly at first before being loud enough that it was clear.

"I'm sorry," the old man said as an audible *click* sound was heard over the speaker.

"Was that a—" Tyler started to ask before the *bang* of a handgun shot through the speaker.

The crying stopped and was replaced by the old man mumbling softly to himself.

"He's praying," Flea said. "He's saying 'Hail Mary' over and over."

Then, without warning, the cassette stopped.

Tyler lifted the frame in his hand and looked it over.

"The man said *look through it*," Loki said.

Tyler nodded and then held the frame at eye level. He slowly looked around the room. Everything looked the same. Looked as you would expect it to look when you peek through a frame into your living room. He slowly moved the frame from left to right until he hovered it over Thomas.

Standing above Thomas was a black shadow. Tyler lowered the frame and looked at Thomas without it. Nothing. He lifted it again, and the shadow was now standing over Thomas's lifeless body. It reached down and dipped its hand into the blood around Thomas's head. It brought the finger back to its mouth and began to suck the blood from its fingers like it was licking melted chocolate on a hot day.

Tyler swallowed hard, "Yeah, I think it's real."

Loki lowered his head, "Fuck."

"What do we do?" Tyler asked.

Flea reached out and grabbed her husband's hand while he looked down at her.

"We do what—"

Tyler didn't hear her finish the thought.

He felt his body lift from the couch and fly through the air, back into the darkness of the house.

Tyler heard his wife and Loki scream, and below that... below the cries of his loved ones, he heard the laughter that was pulling him away from them.

***

Flea stopped mid-sentence.

She felt the words slip from her brain as fast as her husband had slipped away from her.

She felt Loki spring towards Tyler without skipping a beat.

Flea took a moment to realize everything that had happened; then, shaking her head in disbelief, she stood up and gave chase.

She heard Tyler scream for her as she turned the corner and ran into the kitchen.

Loki had been a step ahead of her, but he had stopped.

The kitchen was now nothing but bodies.

Bodies hung on meat hooks.

The smell hit her like a fist to the face. Rotting, spoiling, infected meat. The sound of flies buzzing around her filled her ears. The bodies, all naked, hung with the hook pierced through their chest, the silver tips shining off the kitchen light. Their skin reminded Flea of prepackaged jerky she had literally *just* purchased, from a gas station on the ride home. A ride home that seemed like it was years ago, but couldn't have been more than a couple hours before. Flea had spent hours upon hours in a packed van with her best friends in the world. They laughed about jokes that only the group would understand. Talked about past stories and how someone in the group had once been tricked into smoking meth while being told it was just some kind of fancy marijuana strain. They had focused on intimate stories that they had only talked about within the group, stories about past lovers that would make them feel as if they'd die of embarrassment if anyone outside the group found out. It had been one of her favorite weekends of her life, and now she was here. Standing in front of a collection of what looked like melting bodies. Some of the people had their hands tied behind their backs or in front of them, others were also tied around their ankles. She tried not to focus on their faces, but it was hard not to. They each looked like they died in the most excruciating amount of pain. Like their life had been ripped from them mid-scream.

In the back was an empty hook.

And Tyler on his knees beside it.

Loki reached his hand out and stopped Flea from stepping forward.

"Wait," he said softly.

"Fuck that," Flea said.

"No," Loki said and slowly pointed to the corner of the kitchen. Something within the shadows moved. "It's still here."

Flea looked into the shadows and watched. A female stepped out; her body swaying like she was enjoying the pain she was causing the group. Her dress was tattered and stripped, it looked like she had spent a decade buried beneath the earth. Centipedes and earwigs crawled around her skin and through her ratty hair. Her lips were chapped and cracking, but she smiled through those cracks, which just made them bleed.

Slowly, she swayed towards Tyler.

"Honey!" Flea screamed.

Tyler's head shot up, but Flea could see that he was blindfolded. A gray strap that may have even been ripped from her own dress, was tied around Tyler's eyes. "Don't!" he screamed.

"Babe!" Flea felt the tears welling in her eyes. "Babe! No!"

Tyler shook his head, "Don't. Please don't. Get out of here."

Loki wrapped his arms around Flea and she felt him lock in and tighten his grip around her.

Flea buried her face into his chest and began to once again lose control of her emotions. She heard what sounded like the meat hooks on chains lowering, a slow *tink-tink-tink-tink*. Flea heard Tyler struggle for a minute before the deafening sound of a hook being thrusted into his chest rolled around her. It sounded wet. Violent. Tyler let out a booming scream. Flea covered her ears and flinched. She crushed her eyelids as tightly shut as she could and gritted her teeth. Tyler continued to scream as Flea heard the chains of the meat hook begin to slowly lift him from the ground.

"Tartar-sauce!" Tyler screamed at the top of his lungs.

Flea pulled away from Loki and whipped her head towards her husband.

I love you, he mouthed while blood spilled from his chest and his body slowly went limp.

***

Loki walked Flea back to the front room.

As soon as he had turned her around and held her shoulders, he could smell the scent of rotting flesh disappear as if it was never really there in the first place.

Loki didn't know what to say. There was nothing he *could* say.

He knew exactly how she felt.

He had lost a loved one before.

Watched her die right in front of him.

Then, she came back years later and peeled his calf like a carrot, but that wasn't what he was getting at.

Flea didn't even know what she wanted at this moment and Loki knew that. Her brain was firing a million things all at once, and also held absolutely nothing. Her mind was racing a million miles an hour but was also crashed into a wall. It was a feeling that no one knows until they are in it, and even though Loki had been in it, he still didn't know what she needed.

Instead, he walked her over to the couch and sat down beside her.

"Baby," a familiar voice said from the stairs.

Loki looked away from Flea and saw Arial sitting at the top of the staircase. She tossed an item from hand to hand. Loki concentrated on what it could be, then he realized that it was Shawna's detached jaw. Arial tossed it between her hands like a baseball in the mitts of an anxious teenager. "Baby, come on. We don't have to be done yet."

Loki didn't respond, but he also didn't look away. His attention was now locked in on her.

"Don't go," Flea said. "She's not real."

"I know," Loki responded. "I'm aware. It's just great to see her again, even if this version of her really sucks harder than a hoover vacuum in a frat house."

Loki kept looking up the staircase at the person he once loved more than life itself.

"What does that mean?" Flea asked.

"What?"

"More than a hoover vacuum in a frat house?"

Loki looked down at his friend, "Like… a vacuum… and the hose… and a house full of men. You know?"

Flea smiled even as tears rolled down her face, "No, I don't think I do."

"I–I really don't think I want to finish this joke then," Loki said with a smile.

"Tell me later," Flea said. "Okay?"

"Okay," Loki said and he looked back up to an empty staircase.

She was gone.

In his mind he both feared and hoped that it would be the last time he ever saw her.

"Will it ever stop hurting?" Flea asked with a soft voice that broke Loki's heart once again, taking him back to a point in his life where he had asked the very same question.

Loki shrugged, "Maybe. Someday. I'll let you know if it happens."

The two fell silent. They sat in the room together on the couch and waited for the next awful thing to happen to them. It was an impending doom that he was starting to become familiar with. He had spent so much of his life feeling some form of it, that this was just that feeling turned up to eleven on the dial.

CHAPTER THIRTEEN

THIS ALL ENDS HORRIBLY

Loki lifted up the frame and rotated it in his hand. "What do you want to do?"

Flea shrugged, "I want this to all be over, but I don't think we can walk out of this one, ya know?"

Loki nodded his head in agreement, "You're right. I don't know how we finagle our way out of this. What do we tell the authorities? How do we explain our friends and loved ones being torn to shreds? Best case scenario, we are on the run for the rest of our life; worst case scenario we are in court in an orange jumpsuit."

Flea didn't answer.

"You make the call," Loki said as he handed the frame to Flea.

Flea instantly pushed it away, "Fuck you! This isn't going to be *on me*."

Loki felt the frame shoved into his chest with enough force that he felt his chest audibly *pop*.

"What do you think we should do?" She asked.

Loki thought about it for a moment, "I–I don't know. I don't think I feel right about letting someone else die, because we were afraid to."

Flea smiled at her friend, "Yeah, me neither."

"So what do we do?"

"I don't know," Flea admitted. "However, whatever it is… we figure it out together."

"Hoc finitur Horribly," Flea said as she ran her fingers down one side of the blackened frame. She paused and looked at Loki.

He nodded.

"Hoc finitur violentē," Flea said as she continued down the next side of the frame. "Hoc omne tandem finit."

The final line was harder to read; Flea ran a finger across the edge and smeared some dust from the etched words, "Hoc omnes fines."

Flea didn't know what she expected to happen. Maybe an explosion of light or a *boom* that would shake the house. Maybe she would feel it in her soul, and it would rattle her to her core. But nothing happened.

"Is it done?" Loki asked.

"I–I don't know," Flea said.

Loki looked around the room, "Okay, then let's check."

"How?"

Loki stood up and walked towards the front door.

Flea followed him as strode up to the body of a friend that Flea knew had died, but up until this moment she hadn't seen it… so it didn't fully feel real.

Thomas's face was ripped from his skull. Muscle and fat clung to his bones, and blood dripped and pooled beneath his skull. His eyes were wide and terrified. It hurt her heart.

Loki turned from his fallen friend and towards the door, "If it hasn't worked, whatever is in here will try and stop us, right? It will stop me from escaping."

"I guess," Flea agreed.

"Okay," Loki said as he reached for the doorknob, "let's see what happens."

Loki gripped the doorknob and exhaled a long breath. He twisted the knob slowly until a clear *click* was heard as the door opened.

Both Loki and Flea let out a sigh of relief.

"Okay," Flea said. "Okay, let's go."

Loki closed the door as they both turned back into the room.

CHAPTER *FOURTEEN*

This was it.

If the voice recorder told them anything, it was that they had put a pause on it all for the next three hours. The evil wanted to be spread, to be shared to the next family or group. At one point Loki and Flea spent a chunk of their conversation on who they would give it to, if they needed to. Who *deserved* it. However, neither of them wanted to be responsible for anyone's death. They talked it through only long enough to know that they needed to *pause* the situation before something ripped them to pieces.

Now they had a plan.

A damn good one, in Loki's opinion.

Loki and Flea left the couch and moved towards the garage door. Flea then went into the garage while Loki pulled away and moved into the kitchen.

Flea didn't need to see this part.

He found Tyler's lifeless body on the floor, a giant hole in his chest and blood draining from it, like a hole in a rusty pipe. The hook was gone, and so was the mess of dead bodies that only a bit ago decorated the kitchen. Loki immediately knew that there would be no way they could talk their way out of this. If someone found any of their dead friends, they wouldn't be able to explain it to anyone. How could they explain a giant hole in Tyler's chest? Thomas's face being peeled off? Fuck, even Shawna's jaw being separated from her head. Loki grabbed a blanket from the living room and threw it over Tyler's body.

Flea entered the kitchen, her head looking in the opposite direction, "Is it safe to look?"

Loki looked down at the motionless body covered in a black throw blanket. "I think it would be best if you start in the other room, let me handle this one."

Flea nodded and leaned over to place a red gasoline jug on the ground.

"Let's burn this mother down," she said as she left the room.

Flea was thankful for Loki.

When Flea said she couldn't pass the cursed frame onto someone else, he didn't try and talk her out of it. After that, they came up with the plan.

Burn it all.

Nothing that a little gasoline couldn't handle.

They were going to douse each of their friends in a healthy amount of gasoline, spread some around the house for good measure, and then when they were ready… throw the frame into the roaring flames.

Would it work? Flea wasn't sure.

It was made of wood, so why not?

Loki entered the room and poured some gasoline on Thomas's body.

"We still have to go upstairs," Flea pointed out. "Make sure we have some left."

Loki pulled the jug up and looked upstairs. "What's going to happen to us?"

Flea shrugged as she walked over to Loki, "I don't know. Nothing good, I assume."

"What if us burning it, *saves* us? What if we get to walk away? What do we do then?"

Flea reached for the bottle of gasoline, "Then we adopt new names and run."

"Cool, cool," Loki said. "I'm going to go as… Mike Ock."

Flea chuckled, "Awesome, I'll go as: Dixie. Dixie Rect."

Loki smiled.

It wasn't a real smile. It wasn't the same type of smile that he had on his face throughout the trip. The night had torn him down, ripped out every spark that he had in him. Flea could see it. She knew that he would say the same thing about her.

Together they walked upstairs.

They located their friends and poured the remaining fuel onto them. Then they carefully led a trail of fuel back down the staircase and connected it to the line that Loki had led from Tyler and Thomas.

"Okay," Flea said. "This is it."

"Moment of truth," Loki said.

"Sure is."

"Now we just need a lighter," Loki said.

"Check the drawer on the white cabinet," Flea said, pointing towards it for him. "I know Shawna has one in there for her candles."

She watched Loki turn and open the drawer.

"I've got it," Loki turned around, holding the little white lighter in his hand. He tossed it in the air towards her.

Flea caught it with both hands, before feeling a force pressed up against her back and stomach.

She looked down and saw the tip of a knife poking through her belly.

Then everything went black.

***

Loki watched it.

The lighter in the air, Flea reaching out to grab it, and when she moved, Loki saw someone behind her.

Not just anyone though.

Arial.

A moment later he saw a blade pierce through Flea's stomach, and then Arial smacked Flea in the back of her head. Flea dropped to the floor as the blood pumped from her belly.

Arial stepped forward. "Do you think you guys are the first people to try this idea?"

Loki didn't answer, instead he took a step backwards.

"Come on," Arial said. "Do you think we would just *let* you stop this? That's not how this works. You can either play by the rules and pass us along to the next fucked souls, or you can join your friend on the floor."

"Tough. Tough call to make," Loki nodded his head. "On one hand, I very much enjoy being alive. It's honestly one of my favorite things to be, ya know? On the other hand, I'm not really big on letting my life cost other people theirs. So, I just don't know."

Arial smiled. "Works for me. I was hoping I'd get to have some more one-on-one time with you."

"Pass," Loki said as he reached back into the drawer slowly. "I've already had my fill of your idea of "one-on-one time". I'd rather lick a cheese grater."

"That can be arranged," Arial said as she stepped closer.

Loki moved his hand around as he blindly searched for a second lighter. Shawna didn't just have the one lighter in the drawer, he had seen a couple in there. Finally, his fingers grasped another lighter. Loki pulled it out, and as fast as he could, he sparked it to life.

Arial lunged at him, but not faster than Loki was able to toss the silver zippo lighter into the air and into the line of fuel on the staircase.

A flame exploded on the carpeted stairs.

It jumped both up and down the line of gas.

Arial turned her attention towards the fire, as Loki followed her. Arial stomped on the fire, trying to disrupt the fire from spreading more. Loki threw his body into her, knocking her against the nearest wall. He didn't stop; he grabbed her by both of her shoulders and threw her in the air. She soared through the hallway and into the kitchen like a ragdoll, her head connecting with the countertop with a deep *thud*. He collected himself and sprinted towards her before she could get up from the ground. Loki straddled her and began to throw punches, connecting with her face. He used every inch of his brainspace to push past the fact that he was punching the love of his life, over and over again. He tried to separate himself from what he was doing. What he had to continue to do.

Punch after punch, Loki's fists became more bloodied and swollen. Arial's face began to *pop*. With each punch it began to swell more and more; until the skin stretched too far and split open. However, Arial didn't try and fight back.

Instead, she appeared to be smiling.

"Why the hell are you so happy?" Loki asked between punches.

Arial laughed, "You'll see in a second."

"What does that mean?" Loki asked. He stopped punching and sat up straight.

He could smell the fire ripping through the house. Part of him didn't care. They had won. Flea may be bleeding out, but if Loki could get to her in time, he might be able to get her to safety. Get her out and get her help.

Loki began to run the series of events through his head. She was stabbed. Maybe that would be a good thing. They could tell the authorities they were being held hostage by someone, and that would explain why everyone else was dead. This actually could end with them NOT going to jail.

Arial still smiled up at him.

So, why was she letting the fire eat the house?

Why wasn't she trying to stop the fire?

"So that's the plan?" Loki heard himself say from the living room.

"Yeah, I think so," Loki heard Flea say back.

Loki stood and cautiously walked towards the living room. The TV was on. The room glowed white with the large screen in the otherwise pitch dark room.

"Then let's go," Loki heard himself say on the screen.

He recognized what he was watching.

It was the moment that Loki and Flea decided their plan and acted upon it. He watched them walk together to the garage and then watched her go in and retrieve the gas can. The television then followed her as she walked into the kitchen and they continued the conversation, as Loki had just finished putting the blanket on Tyler's body. Then he watched as Flea placed the gasoline can on the ground and walked away, same as Loki remembered it.

Loki watched the scene on the television. It was strange, watching it all back. Loki walked up and picked up the gas can, bringing it over towards Tyler's dead body.

Loki looked away from the TV and to Tyler's actual body, not too far from him. The black blanket was still draped over his body; the smell, a mixture of nickel from the blood and gas fumes, floated through the air.

He looked back at the television and watched himself walk over to the body. He tipped the gas can, but nothing came out. The lid was still on the can.

"What?" Loki said to himself.

Arial walked around the corner and leaned against the wall, "Sorry."

"We didn't actually pour the gasoline, did we?" Loki asked.

"Keep watching."

Loki could still smell the fire.

He saw it explode in front of him on the staircase.

Was all of that in his head too?

He turned back towards the television.

Loki watched himself pour the gasoline line down the staircase, only this time he had seen himself remove the lid. The fuel poured out on the carpet as he slowly walked backwards down the staircase and onto the ground.

"Okay," Flea said. "This is it."

"Moment of truth," Loki said.

"Sure is."

Loki watched in horror as he saw himself lift the gas can and begin to pour fuel over Flea. She didn't seem to notice. Her hair absorbed the fuel and it ran down her body and into the bloodstained clothing.

They continued talking as if nothing was happening. "Now we just need a lighter," Loki said.

"Check the drawer on the white cabinet," Flea said

"No," Loki said to Arial. "This isn't what happened."

Arial smiled.

Loki sprinted from the living room and past Arial, through the kitchen and down the hallway. Loki could still smell the fire, the smoke filling the hallway as he approached where he had last seen Flea.

The line that he thought Arial was trying to tap out, (but she had really used to distract Loki and pull him away from the real situation), was slowly burning; dying out as it had eaten most of the fuel.

Then he found Flea.

Her body was lying on the ground, a knife in her stomach, and flames covering her entire body.

***

Loki tried to put the fire out.

He grabbed a blanket from the couch and tried to smother the flame.

It didn't work.

The flame continued to burn her to a crisp.

Her skin was blackened. The smell of burning skin and hair infiltrated his nostrils.

Loki fell to his knees.

They had lost.

After all of this… it was useless.

"Oh, I'm sorry, baby," Arial said as she walked into the room. Loki didn't look over at her, but in his peripheral vision he could see she was holding something shiny. "I thought you knew."

Loki didn't answer.

Arial walked over to him, lifting him by his shirt collar from the floor. "We aren't done here."

Loki looked at her. He had nothing left in him. He could feel it. His fight was over.

Arial held a cheese grater in front of him, "Remember… we have plans."

Loki looked at the silver cheese grater as Arial held it towards his face, "Fine," he said. "Can I at least sit on the couch? Maybe?"

Arial smiled. "Get comfortable while I work?"

"Whatever," Loki said. "Let's just get this over with."

Loki walked over to the couch, Arial trailing behind him.

There it was.

Right where they had left it.

Loki reached out to the coffee table and recovered the frame.

In one swift motion he snapped it over his knee.

He felt his body thrown to the side as Arial ripped into him.

He stumbled to the ground, but recovered, pushing her back off.

Loki crawled to the broken frame he had broken into two pieces.

He felt Arial struggling to grab him, finally using her sharp nails on his open wound that she had given him with the potato peeler. Loki screamed as the sharp pain shot throughout his body; Arial's fingernails dug deep inside his bloody wound.

Still, he continued to crawl. Loki picked up the pieces of the frame and smashed the frame over and over on the ground. It splintered and split into smaller and smaller pieces.

No one would ever see it again.

This was going to end.

Arial released him.

Loki stopped and tried to catch his breath.

The only sounds in the house were his own breathing and of the fire beside him, cooking one of his best friends.

Loki rolled over, feeling his chest rise and fall.

All of the weight of the night left his body. He smiled.

He knew what was about to come.

Arial stepped over him, the cheese grater still in her hand.

"I'm all yours, honey," he said as he stuck his tongue out at her.

CHAPTER FIFTEEN

THIS ALL ENDS HORRIBLY

Joseph hated this part of the job.

He was part of a crew that was hired to go in and clean up messes that no one else wanted to. Usually it was to clean up a suicide or a freak accident that the family were too depressed or traumatized to deal with.

This one was different though.

Seven people, brutally tortured and murdered in a house.

The FBI were called in, pictures were taken, pages and pages of information was collected. It baffled everyone. News outlets reported it. Theories were thrown about, but at the end of the day there wasn't anyone arrested. No suspects. Nothing.

Now, several long months later, Joseph was scrubbing blood from the wall upstairs. There used to be two dead bodies here. Joseph could tell by the large pools of dried blood that there had been two separate bodies here at one time.

"Joey!" Joseph heard Ashley yell for him from downstairs.

Joseph dropped the sponge into the bucket of disgusting water, wiped his hands on his pant legs, and headed downstairs.

Ashley was in between the dining room and front room.

This was where the most blood had been. Someone was ripped to shreds in here. Blood spread against the hardwood floor and every inch of the walls around. Chunks of hair and flesh stuck to the dried blood. Joseph had read somewhere online that the man had been tortured for hours; until his body was nothing more than scraps, exposed muscles, and fat.

"What's up?" Joseph asked.

"Check this out," Ashley said as she showed Joseph what was in her hands. "Neat, huh?"

Joseph looked at it, "What is it?"

"Looks like something we could sell," Ashley said.

It wouldn't be the first time they'd snuck something out and sold it on eBay. People paid top dollar for something macabre that was plucked from an actual murder site.

"You think we could fix it?" Ashley asked.

Joseph looked at it, "What is it?"

"I think it's some kind of picture frame?"

The fucking horrible end

ACKNOWLEDGMENTS

I would like to thank some people for making this book happen, in no particular order. I'm very sorry if I've left anyone out that belongs in this section of the book, know this part of the book is the hardest for me because I don't want to leave ANYONE out!

    First, I would like to thank my family. I have been blessed with such an amazing group of cheerleaders and it makes me want to pump out as many books as possible so they can see how it is possible to do things that other people want to do. I want them to reach for their goals and take chances that might not work out, but they will be proud that they gave it their all. My kids are insanely motivated at art and anything creative, I want them to have a support structure that rewards that. And me putting them at the end of a book is just a small portion of what I can do to show them I'm proud of them. So... Justin, Kyky, Lenny, Roz... Dad loves you and couldn't be more proud that I am your father.

    Secondly, I wanted to thank Robyn and Tyler for everything they've done for me in my journey as an author. When I needed to find a way to travel out of town, they were always letting me crash with them and helped out with extra cash flow that wasn't at all necessary (but was none the less appreciated). Even beyond my writing you've both been a support structure for me that I have no had in my life and I can't thank you enough for being there for me all this time. My kids love you and cherish the relationship you have created and there is literally nothing better in my opinion than someone who loves my children.

Thank you to a certain group of friends that meet up at our house once a week. I promised you guys that you would become main players in a book at some point... and here it is. My first attempt at splatter horror and seeing how the girls love horror as much as I do... I thought it was right. I hope the story lives up to your expectations and that everyone is *semi*-happy with how their characters met their fate.

Thank you to Loki DeWitt. This motherfucker has been with me through thick and thin. Writing comic books, running a bloody comic book publishing house by mistake, making the jump to novels... he has been there. Even when things got weird and I got hurt and didn't talk to anyone for months... he was always in my inbox checking in. I love you, bro. Thanks for being there.

A special thanks to Mr. Cody Kendall. This guy was asked for pictures for a simple "WANTED" poster and that someone turned a wheel in my brain and I dragged it out through all the QR codes in the book. I then had to ask him to find a way to shoot the small video and was dedicated enough to the idea to beg him to do so... he didn't hesitate and did it the same night. Seriously, an amazing friend and I don't deserve people like this in my life.

Thank you to all my spooky friends on social media that helped me out by reading and blurbing my book. I know I gave them almost no time to read it and so many people stepped up and helped me out! I am insanely grateful and will return the favor if ever needed. Thank you to some of my awesome readers, I would like to call some people out that have been insanely helpful on spreading the word about my books in a way that putting their name in this part is the least I could do: Alysha Yuhas, Holly K Hummel, Alyssa Cook, Lisa Breanne, Allia Kennedy, Jules Weinman, and countless others that I feel bad that I can't continue... but I have to cut it off somewhere. Thank you for reading, sharing, pushing my books. It is so cool of you all and I appreciate it so much.

A thank you to Timothy King. Dude helped me find an editor when I was honestly trying to get information from him on a completely different one. I am so happy I somehow stumbled across his page on TikTok, and can't thank him enough for helping me.

To my freaking ALL-STAR of an editor, Meriah Gutterson at Marked up Editing. I really am impressed by how fast you edited and how accurate you were. I loved how you jumped right in and gave me some very important advice on how to make the book stronger. Without you the ending would have been completely different and would have gotten me a lot of 1 star reviews. I'm gonna make sure you are on whatever book I self publish from here on out.

ABOMINATION MEDIA

ABOUT THE AUTHOR

Mike Salt is the author of several horror novels, including *The Linkville Horror Series* and *Price Manor: The House That Burns* and this thing you just read. Mike is not a raccoon, although some people in the writing community are trying to make that claim. He has never gone through a neighbors trash can and taken his small (normal sized) hands and shoved a handful of trash into his furry mouth. He wishes that people would leave him alone and let him be. He has things to do and people are getting in way of completing his goals. Mike only writes his books at night, no, I know you are thinking: "Well, hell, a raccoon is nocturnal, so maybe *he is* a raccoon." He is not. He just has a billion offspring and they keep him busy throughout the day. Mike also enjoys nachos.

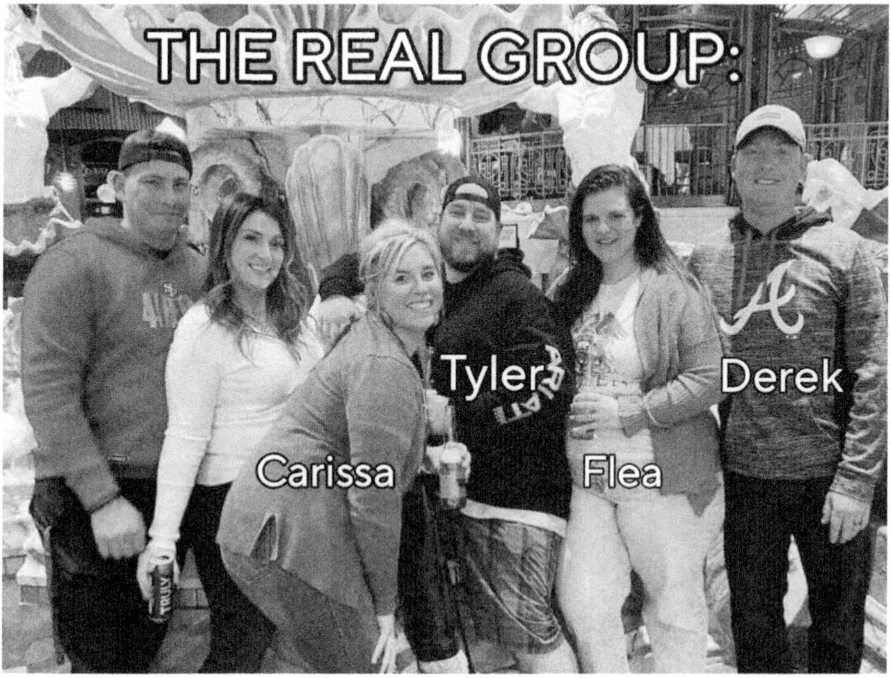
THE REAL GROUP:
Tyler
Derek
Carissa
Flea

CONTENT WARNINGS

Blood

Violence

Abduction

Murder

Coulrophobia

Child endangerment

Catoptrophobia

Tension breaking jokes

Bibliophobia

Necrophobia

Nomophobia

Phobophobia

Pyrophobia

Heights

FINAL CODE

THIS ALL ENDS HORRIBLY | 128

Printed in Great Britain
by Amazon